The Double Life
of Liliane

Also by Lily Tuck

The Double Life of Liliane

a novel

Lily Tuck

Atlantic Monthly Press
New York

Published simultaneously in Canada
Printed in the United States of America

FIRST EDITION

ISBN 978-0-8021-2402-9
eISBN 978-0-8021-9089-5

Atlantic Monthly Press
an imprint of Grove Atlantic
154 West 14th Street
New York, NY 10011

Distributed by Publishers Group West

groveatlantic.com

15 16 17 18   10 9 8 7 6 5 4 3 2 1

To my grandmother, Lily Solmsen, who told me stories
And to Elisabeth Schmitz who made them better

Part fact part fiction is what life is. And it is always a cover story.
I wrote my way out.

—Jeanette Winterson

I believe one has a public life, a private life and a secret life.
I have written a lot about my public and private lives.
On my secret life, I have not written a single word.

—Gabriel García Márquez

The Double Life
of Liliane

Prologue

As a child I am often sick. Something to do with my heart. Pale, I lie on the examining table, with only a sheet to half hide my nakedness, as Dr. Fischer presses his cold stethoscope against my ribs and tells me to breathe.

"Breathe normally," he says.

Then, "Take a deep breath. Again."

Dr. Fischer is old. His hands shake a little and are covered with brown spots.

He listens.

Lub—the first heart sound is the closing of the atrioventricular valves.

Dub—the second heart sound is the closing of the semilunar valves.

Lub dub lub dub lub dub lub dub lub dub lub dub

Dr. Fischer listens for *lud dub ta*—a protodiastolic gallop sound—and for *ta lub dub*—an atrial gallop sound. He also listens for heart murmurs that make a whooshing sound generated by a turbulent flow of blood. These can be benign or they can be abnormal.

Dr. Fischer is a kind if not entirely gentle man. His eyesight is failing, perhaps the reason he is awkward and a bit rough. The way he presses too hard on my collarbone.

"An innocent murmur," he informs me.

I am a little afraid of Dr. Fischer, but I summon up the courage to ask him: "Am I going to die?"

"No." Then, reconsidering, he pats my arm and says, "Yes, but not for a long time."

I

Liliane's double life begins at New York's Idlewild Airport when she boards a Trans World Airlines L-749 Constellation, the first commercial plane to cross the Atlantic nonstop thanks to its additional fuel tanks. The flight from New York to Rome usually takes from fourteen to sixteen hours depending on the wind, but on account of engine trouble, the flight Liliane takes is longer. The passengers are made to disembark and wait in Gander for several hours—the airport is a metal Quonset hut with no shops or cafeteria—until another plane arrives. As Liliane gets ready to board a second time, too late, she remembers that she left the cardboard box with the cheesecake in the overhead compartment above her seat in the first plane. A day earlier, she and her mother had bought the cheesecake at a delicatessen on Fifty-eighth Street as a gift for her father. It was to have been a surprise. A few days before Christmas, it has begun to snow heavy wet flakes in Gander. How old is she then? Nine? Ten? She is wearing a red coat and she does not want to go to Rome.

Already, Liliane misses her mother. Her beautiful mother whose looks have been compared to Greta Garbo's and Marlene Dietrich's. One time, when Liliane's mother got lost looking for the Third Avenue Bridge in Manhattan in order to avoid paying the toll on the Triborough, a policeman stopped her and, after taking a good look at her, asked if she was Marlene Dietrich and Liliane's mother replied that if she was Marlene Dietrich she would not be driving out of her way and getting lost to save twenty-five cents.

Liliane does not look like her mother, she looks like her father.

When next the plane lands, the sun is out and it is the bright following day. They have crossed the Atlantic and are in Shannon, Ireland. Looking out the window as the plane taxis, Liliane catches a glimpse of a rabbit in the grass along the runway. At the sound of the plane, the rabbit stands on its hind legs, then turning, hops quickly away.

In the terminal, Liliane walks back and forth looking at the shops. In one, a souvenir shop, a four-leaf clover inside a round plastic charm dangling from a key chain catches her eye. A good luck charm. All of a sudden, she wants it, only she has no money. The saleslady is busy making change for a customer who has bought a wool cap and, on an impulse, Liliane takes the four-leaf clover key chain. The saleslady must suspect something for she looks up as Liliane is slipping the key chain into the pocket of her red coat, but just then the customer who bought the wool cap says something to the saleslady and she gets distracted.

The passenger seated next to Liliane is a middle-aged man who, during the flight, smokes, drinks several glasses of scotch, and is friendly. He tells her that he has a little girl who must be about the same age as Liliane and that her name is Jennifer. Jennifer wants a special kind of doll for Christmas, the man tells Liliane. A doll baby who drinks, wets, and says *mama*. The man speaks a lot more about Jennifer—what she does and what she says—and it soon becomes apparent to Liliane that Jennifer is quite a bit younger than she and Liliane loses interest in her. She falls asleep, and during the layover in Paris, she is asleep in her seat—she has not taken off her red coat and her hand is in the pocket, holding the key chain with the four-leaf clover charm attached to it. She is unaware that the passenger next to her has disembarked or that there has been a change in the crew. The new stewardess who has come on board does not want to wake her.

Jennifer is eating great mouthfuls of cheesecake. Her face is covered with cheesecake, some of it has gotten into her hair. "Stop!" Liliane shouts at her, she is close to tears. "Stop!" she shouts again, "the cheesecake is for my father!"

Liliane is still sleeping when they get ready to land at Ciampino, Rome's airport, named after the commune of Ciampino, which in turn was named for Giovanni Giustino Ciampini, a seventeenth-century ecclesiastical archaeologist. Had Liliane been awake she might have seen, out of her window, how the plane flies directly over the ruins of several Roman aqueducts. And had she been a little older and studied Roman history at school, she might have known how by the fourth century BC, due to the rapid growth of the population and thus the need for a greater water supply, the Romans had begun to build aqueducts that carried water all the way from springs in the Apennine Mountains. In addition, she might have known how by then the Romans had also figured out that the aqueducts' gradient had to be about a one-foot drop per two hundred feet in length so that the water could flow fast enough but not too fast to wash out of the aqueduct.

The stewardess, a pretty blonde, tries to brush out the wrinkles on Liliane's red coat and to adjust the plastic barrette that holds Liliane's hair in place as she gets ready to leave the plane.

"Did you bring a hat, little girl?" the pretty blonde stewardess asks. "You haven't forgotten anything?" (Later, the stewardess will tell the handsome co-pilot she is sleeping with how, to her way of thinking, it is nearly criminal of the parents to let a child so young fly by herself. She will say this as she adjusts the little gray cap adorned with a silver badge in the shape of a wing on her neatly coiffed blonde head. And, furthermore, she continues, smiling now, if she herself were, one day, to have children, she would never ever let them travel alone.)

The next day, during the layover, while the co-pilot and the pretty stewardess are crossing Piazza Venezia on their way to the Forum, they helplessly watch as a young man drives by on a Vespa and grabs a woman's purse, knocking her to the ground.

"Oh, my god," the stewardess says, as she starts to take a step toward the woman.

"It could have been you," the co-pilot says, taking her arm and pulling her along to the Forum.

"I think I hate Rome," the stewardess says.

*   *   *

Liliane's father, Rudy, has furnished the guest room in his Rome apartment with her in mind: the bed, the armoire, the bureau are little and painted white (and, for the next eight or nine years that she will come visit, the furniture in the room will remain the same). The apartment is in a modern seven-story building located on Via San Crescenziano, a small street named after Saint Crescentinus. A Roman soldier, Saint Crescentinus had converted to Christianity and was said to have slain a dragon, which led to many conversions. Nonetheless, in AD 303, he was beheaded. He is the patron saint of the city of Urbino and his relics are supposed to cure supplicants of their headaches. Via San Crescenziano runs into Via Salaria, which stretches across the entire width of Italy, from Porto d'Ascoli on the Adriatic coast all the way to Rome. Via Salaria is so named because the road was originally used by the Sabines to transport *sal* (Latin for salt) from the Roman saltworks at the mouth of the Tiber to their home in the Apennines. At present, Via Salaria joins highway SS4, which, in turn, joins highway A1, the *Autostrada del Sole*, the longest of Italy's highways—the 754 kilometers connect Milan via Bologna, Florence, and Rome with Naples. Also, since Liliane's father's apartment is not far from the open countryside, prostitutes line Via Salaria, at all hours of the day and night, waiting for customers to pick them up.

In the living room, the blue velvet sofa, the green glass coffee table, the two matching stuffed chairs, and her father's ornate mahogany desk are all new. Except for a large Venetian glass ashtray on top of the coffee table—her father smokes a pack of cigarettes a day, Chesterfields he buys on the black market— there are no books or magazines or other objects to give the room a lived-in look. The only personal object in the room is the statue of a lion that sits on her father's desk. It is the Golden Laurel Award he received at the Venice Film Festival in 1950 for a film called *Donne senza Nome* (*Women without Names*) starring Simone Simon and Françoise Rosay and set after World War II, in a displaced persons' camp, where the lives and freedom of three women and a newborn child are at stake. The actresses playing the women detainees speak in many different languages—Italian, English, French, Serbo-Croatian, and German—and the film's location scenes were shot in Puglia, in the town of Alberobello, famous for its distinctive houses with cone-shaped stone roofs. A few years later, Rudy will put a framed photo of Liliane next to the statue of the lion. The photo—a photo she does not like (it looks posed and her hair at the time is too short)—will be taken by a well-known photographer, who is a friend both of her father and of Marilyn Monroe. (The photographer and his wife are also friends of Audrey Hepburn and the photographer's wife likes to tell Liliane how, at lunch one day, when she was heavily pregnant, she asked Audrey Hepburn not to take off her coat and reveal her tiny waist and Audrey Hepburn didn't.)

A terrace off the living room gives on to Villa Ada. Originally owned by the House of Savoy, the Italian royal family, a large part of the park is public and boasts an artificial lake and many different types of trees, including a rare Tibetan metasequoia. At Liliane's father's request, the maid, Maria, has bought a few plants for the terrace—bougainvillea and geraniums—and she waters them daily, careful to make sure that the water does not spill over onto the terrace below. When Liliane is older—instead of coming to visit her father at Christmas, she comes in the summer for the month of July—she spends hours out on the terrace sunbathing in her bikini. From there, too—if she stands at the far end of the terrace—Liliane can see into the windows of the apartment of the building next door. The apartment belongs to Gualtiero Jacopetti, the dashingly handsome director of *Mondo Cane*, the controversial film made up of a series of lurid and macabre scenes—a woman in New Guinea suckling a baby pig, risky rituals involving poisonous snakes, the running of the bulls in Pamplona with people getting gored. The film was nominated for several awards and spawned several sequels known as "shockumentaries." As for Gualtiero Jacopetti, in 1955 he was jailed for having had sex with a fourteen-year-old Gypsy girl named Jolanda Calderas, whom he was later forced to marry.

Leaning out of his apartment window, Gualtiero is watching Liliane as she sunbathes.

"How old are you?" he asks her.

In the morning, before her father leaves for work, he and Liliane breakfast in the dining room. Her father has a hearty appetite and eats a large meal—coffee, milk, bread, butter, ham, cheese, and fruit. She and her father, who is from Germany originally, speak French together.

"Papa" is what she calls him.

French is Liliane's first language, but, since at home now she speaks only English; her French is rusty and she finds it harder to express herself in it. In addition—and she will find this to always be true—she feels like a different person speaking French and not like her ordinary self. The difference is hard to explain but whether she speaks French or English at breakfast makes little difference. Busy eating, Liliane and her father are mostly silent.

Maria, the maid, serves them. Maria is short, dark, and unobtrusive. She makes up the beds, washes, cleans, shops for Liliane's father and, in turn, for Liliane, when she is there. Since at first Liliane does not speak Italian, she cannot communicate with Maria. She can only say *grazie* and *buon giorno* and *arrividerla*. She does not know anything about Maria—whether she is married, a widow, or has children, or, perhaps, even grandchildren. Nor does she know how old Maria is. As far as Liliane is concerned, Maria could be any age. Even when Liliane is older and has learned to speak Italian, she still learns nothing about Maria or Maria's life. Liliane's father knows nothing about her either, or, only, that Maria is honest—*onestà*.

After Liliane's father leaves to go to work, Maria goes to the market and Liliane is alone. It is not clear what she does for the next three or four hours—hours that she has no memory of—until Maria returns and telephones for a taxi to take Liliane to meet her father at his office.

Pronto! Pronto!—Hello! Hello!

Liliane can hear Maria shout into the telephone, repeating the address, then the directions: *dopo Piazza Priscilla*—after Piazza Priscilla—*prima da Piazza Viscovio*—before Piazza Viscovio.

Subito . . . subito—right away . . . right away, she also entreats.

Very often, Liliane has to wait a long time outside her father's apartment building before the taxi arrives. Very often, too, the taxi does not arrive and Liliane has to go back upstairs and Maria has to telephone a second time.

Pronto! Pronto! Maria starts up again.

Her father's office is located on Corso d'Italia, an avenue that runs parallel to a section of the Aurelian Wall, known as the Muro Torto (Twisted Wall), which extends through the Villa

Borghese from Via Veneto to Piazza del Popolo. According to one popular legend—of which there are many—the place where the wall stands marks the spot from which Saint Peter defended Rome. Another less savory account claims that the wall was the burial site for robbers, whores, and rebels—among the latter, two men were decapitated in 1852 and, apparently, their ghosts can be seen from time to time holding their bloody heads in their hands. Less dramatic but no less irritating to the drivers, cars are said to invariably run out of gas when approaching the wall. Liliane's father's office is on the top floor of the building and although there is an elevator, the elevator requires a coin to operate it; since the elevator is old, the necessary coins are no longer in circulation, and Liliane's father has to go out of his way to a special bank to buy them. As a result, everyone who works in the office, except for occasionally Liliane's father, who suffers from attacks of gout, walks up the five flights of stairs. The office has high ceilings and is spacious and sunny; the walls are hung with colorful framed posters advertising the films Liliane's father has produced.

Liliane father's real name is Rudolf—only he gives it the French spelling, Rodolphe, and goes by his nickname, Rudy. Rudolf was both a family name and a popular Christian name at the time of his birth, made still more popular by the tragic circumstances of the archduke's death in 1889. Known as the Mayerling incident—named after the archduke's hunting lodge in the Vienna woods where the apparent murder-suicide took place—the deaths of the Crown Prince Rudolf of Austria and his seventeen-year-old mistress, Baroness Marie Vetsera caused a huge international incident, fueled conspiracy theories, and, more important, contributed to the demise of the Hapsburg Empire by destabilizing the immediate line of succession. An only son, Archduke Rudolf had no heir and the succession was passed on to his cousin, Archduke Franz Ferdinand, which triggered further divisions between the Austrian and Hungarian factions of the empire and led to the assassination of Archduke Franz Ferdinand and his wife, Sophie, at Sarajevo in June 1914—"the shot [actually two shots] that was heard round the world," as the saying goes—and a cause for the start of the First World War.

Rudy was born in Bonn; later, he studied in Berlin. In 1933, he left Germany for Paris, claiming that, as a Jew—albeit an assimilated one—he was no longer allowed to play field hockey at his sports club. In Paris, he established a film production company and married Liliane's mother. Together, they lived more or less—often less—happily in a large apartment in the Sixteenth Arrondissement on Rue Raynouard (named after a dull French Academician, who mistakenly wrote that the Romance languages were not derived from Latin) and had a child, Liliane.

On September 3, 1939, two days after the invasion of Poland, when both Britain and France declared war on Germany, everything changed in Rudy's life. All German and Austrian men between the ages of eighteen and fifty living in France were rounded up and put into detention camps, their assets were frozen, their papers confiscated. Imprisoned at first in the Stade de Colombes, the site of the 1924 Olympics, Rudy described the conditions in the stadium in a memoir he wrote many years later about his wartime experience:

> *I brought along a sleeping bag, a rubber mattress, and*
> *a bit of food. A good thing I had taken these elementary*

precautions because the organization in Colombes was nonexistent—no one knew how to proceed. . . . Each new arrival received a number and was sent to find a place in the grandstand of the stadium—the Germans on the right, the Austrians on the left. To use the lavatories or to set foot on the lawn was strictly forbidden; at best, one could walk on the path around the lawn. The "toilets" were the most disgusting things I had ever seen: iron barrels placed perpendicular and at random, into which people relieved themselves. . . . Right away I decided to eat as little as possible so that my use of those barrels would be as infrequent as possible.

After fifteen days in the Stade de Colombes, Rudy and his fellow detainees were put on a bus and quickly driven through the streets of Paris to the Gare d'Austerlitz. On the way, Rudy wrote, "I took a last nostalgic look at the Champs-Elysées, which seemed to be singularly sad and lifeless." From Paris, he was sent to a camp in Marolles, a village in the Loire Valley, seven kilometers from Blois, the town from where Joan of Arc launched her battle to free the city of Orléans. After spending his first night in Marolles inside a barn, Rudy continued:

I awoke feeling quite gloomy; I told myself that if they had forgotten about us at Colombes, here we were even farther away—the refugees were only a small problem for the French Government, or perhaps not even a problem—and to have brought us so far must mean that we would stay here a long time, maybe for the entire duration of the war. My gloomy thoughts were interrupted by a young man who came up to me and asked: Would you like two fried eggs with your breakfast?

I thought he was pulling my leg and I answered him in kind:
Sure, with pleasure! Ten minutes later, I got those eggs. Simon
Herbst, a little Pole, who had nothing to do with the Germans,
except that his papers, due to a bureaucratic mix-up, said
"German national," was an egg merchant in Paris as well
as the most resourceful person I met during the entire war.
Already, he knew everything there was to know about the vil-
lage of Marolles and he was always in a good mood and ready
to help. He made my life in camp much easier. Unfortunately,
he did not stay as resourceful to the bitter end; Simon Herbst
was one of the six million who never came back.

Elected by the 120 detainees, Rudy was made both head
of the Marolles camp and spokesman to the French authorities.
Luckily, the commander of the camp, an old lieutenant, was
disposed to turn a blind eye if one of the prisoners broke the
rules by strolling down the village street or by stopping at the
only café to have a glass of wine. And, according to his memoir,
Rudy must have done a fairly good job as head of the camp:

I never had to deal with any serious uprising, on the
contrary—as a sign of affection, I was asked by one of the
men to be a witness at his wedding. On Sundays, I was so
tired out from all the discussions and petty quarrels, that I
would go to church to have some peace and quiet for an hour.
Every fifteen days or so, my business associate would come
from Paris to see me and, once, he even arranged to have my
wife come and visit me. None of the guards said anything
when that night I did not sleep on the straw in the barn, but,
in the morning, I was on time for the roll call.

After two months at Marolles, the day arrived when the much longed and waited for call finally came: Rudy was free to enlist in the Foreign Legion for the duration of the war in France and not, as had been originally stipulated by the recruitment officer, for the obligatory five years. (The alternative was being deported back to Germany.) Nonetheless, although relieved to leave the camp, Rudy was apprehensive:

> *My whole life growing up in Germany, I had always heard horrible stories about the Foreign Legion. . . . The Foreign Legion was portrayed as made up of murderers and thieves, and life in the Legion was like hell on earth, where certain death awaited one at the end. And this was the Legion I was going to join now—no longer quite so young (I was over thirty with a wife and child), no longer so tough (I was twenty kilos overweight since I had abandoned the sporting life several years ago), and here I was a film producer with a sedentary life and a taste for luxury!*

From Fort St. Jean in Marseille, picturesquely located at the entrance of the old harbor, the place from which, traditionally, legionnaires embark for the unknown, Rudy was sent to Sidi Bel Abbès, in Algeria. Before leaving France, he took note of the large sign placed at the entrance of the fort that read: *Legionnaire, tu es venu pour mourir et je t'envoie où on meurt*—Legionnaire, you have come to die and I am sending you to where one dies.

Then, from Sidi Bel Abbès, Rudy was stationed in Maghnia, a Berber town located in northwestern Algeria, a few miles from the Spanish Moroccan border on the edge of the barren High Plateaus. There, for five months, Rudy led the life of a real legionnaire. He learned how to bear arms and march under the hot African sun to the tune of the popular Foreign Legion song:

> *Auprès de ma blonde,*
> *Qu'il fait bon, fait bon, fait bon.*
> *Auprès de ma blonde,*
> *Qu'il fait bon dormir.*
> *Next to my blonde girl,*
> *How good it is, how good, how good.*
> *Next to my blonde girl,*
> *How good it is to sleep*

During the five months he spent in Maghnia, Rudy lost weight, got into shape, and made friends: the pastry cook at Maxim's, a hardened criminal released from prison on the condition that he serve in the Legion, a musician who called himself Alex Stone and later composed a haunting and hugely popular song called "C'est Fini," "It Is Finished" (the title was misunderstood to be "Symphonie"), as he thought he was about to be shot by the Germans. At night, Rudy played gin rummy and drank the cheap but good local Algerian rosé wine, but best of all as he wrote:

> I look back on this time with pride. I would not have missed it for anything in the world. The Legion gave me something for the rest of my life, not just a good conscience that I did my duty—the fact that I never saw any action was not my fault, I would have liked to, but few Frenchmen did during this lightning-quick war of 1940. I came out of the Legion with a self-assurance and feeling of stability that I did not have before. . . . It was at the Legion that I became a real man.

After the war, Liliane's father became a naturalized French citizen and, soon after that, he left France to live in Rome, "the Eternal City," about to be transformed by Cinecittà—Cinema City—into "Hollywood on the Tiber." Already, by the early 1950s, a number of American production companies, profiting from cheap Italian labor, had begun shooting their films at Cinecittà— films that later included *Ben-Hur*, *Helen of Troy*, and *Cleopatra*. As, of course, so did the Italian directors—Rossellini, Antonioni, Fellini—in particular, Fellini, whose famous film *La Dolce Vita* epitomized the glamorous and often scandalous lives of the stars and would-be stars.

Meanwhile, however, compared to the privileged lives of those involved in the movie industry, the Italian working class was suffering mass unemployment and poverty. In 1952, according to statistics, almost one hundred thousand Romans were homeless or still living in shacks, caves, cellars, or in the *borgate*, the squalid shantytowns built on the outskirts of the capital. (Ironically, until 1947, Cinecittà served as a refugee camp and was the site where Rossellini's *Roma città aperta* was filmed.) Several years later, Pier Paolo Pasolini's film *Accatone!* would perfectly capture the harsh and violent lives of the Roman poor.

In Rome, Rudy drives an expensive sports car, a silver Lancia Spider. The Lancia has a right-hand wheel drive—a feature designed for racing that, as Liliane will discover, is dangerous, since the passenger sitting on the left has a clearer view of the road and of the oncoming traffic than the driver. Instead of a backseat, there is an uncomfortable narrow shelf that Liliane has to crouch on if ever her father takes along another passenger. At midday, the Via Veneto is crowded and there are no parking places. Miraculously, or so it seems to Liliane, a little man comes running out of a side street, waving his cap and yelling, "*Pronti, pronti, dottore!*"—Ready, ready, sir!—the same little man from whom Rudy buys the black market Chesterfields—and Liliane's father hands him the keys to the Lancia.

Liliane's father lunches at Bricktop. Named for its owner, a redheaded African American singer born Ada Beatrice Queen Victoria Louise Virginia Smith, Bricktop was originally located in Paris and was F. Scott Fitzgerald, Ernest Hemingway, John Steinbeck, and Cole Porter's favorite nightclub. In fact, Cole Porter wrote "Miss Otis Regrets" based on a story Bricktop once told him about a lynching in the American South, adding, "Well, that man won't lunch tomorrow." In the early fifties, Bricktop moved to Rome, where it catered to the movie crowd: Elizabeth Taylor, Richard Burton, Ava Gardner, Frank Sinatra, and to Liliane's father, who regularly goes there to play cards—Rudy plays gin rummy and almost always wins—and to eat American-style hamburgers.

Smiling, Bricktop asks Liliane, "Are you going to be a movie star and make your daddy proud?" The perfect hostess, she comes and sits at their table for a few minutes and chats with Liliane's father. Her face is covered with freckles and Liliane cannot help but stare.

After lunch, Liliane's father takes her to a museum—the Villa Borghese or the Doria Pamphili. He is genuinely interested in art and he would like Liliane to be interested as well. He points out paintings, frescoes, sculptures, and Liliane makes an effort to listen. The museums tire her, but she looks forward to visiting the souvenir shops. She wants to get postcards to send to her mother and her school friends and she asks her father to buy them for her.

Or they visit a famous church. Santa Maria in Aracoeli, the Church of the Altar of Heaven, appropriately named, is located on the summit of the Capitoline Hill. Every Christmas a wooden baby Jesus, carved from an olive tree in the Garden of Gethsemene and covered in jewels, is brought out to receive the children's prayers. The baby Jesus does not interest Liliane and the only prayer she knows by heart—*Now I lay me down to sleep, I pray the Lord my soul to keep*—is not appropriate. What she likes best about the church are the 124 steps that lead up to it. Counting them under her breath, she likes to hop first on one foot then on the other all the way up and then all the way down again.

"Be careful," her father calls out to her.

Rudy is not accustomed to looking after a little girl. He does not know what to do with her all day.

He does not know what to say to her.

What are you studying in school?

Do you have a best friend?

Likewise, Liliane does not know what to say to her father.

We are studying the Egyptians.

My best friend is Margo Maximov.

No doubt Rudy would like to ask Liliane different questions:

Is your mother happily married to her new husband?

Do you like your new stepfather?

But he doesn't.

Liliane's father takes her to the Fontana dei Quatro Fiumi on Piazza Navona. Created by Bernini, he explains, the fountains represent the four rivers that symbolize the four quarters of the world: the Danube for Europe, the Nile for Africa, the Ganges for Asia, and the River Plate for South America. What stays in Liliane's head is the story he tells her of how Bernini positioned the cowering figure of a man—his arm held high in the air for protection, an anguished look on his face—on top of the River Plate fountain to show that the figure feared the Church of St. Agnes, built opposite, by Bernini's rival, Borromini, would crumble and fall on top of him. As it turned out, the story is apocryphal since the fountain was built before Borromini built the church.

On Piazza Navona, her father buys her an ice cream cone, *cioccolato e fragola*—chocolate and strawberry—but, soon after eating it, Liliane vomits the ice cream in the street, the chocolate staining the front of her red coat.

At the Fontana di Trevi, Liliane's father hands her a coin, telling her that in order to return to Rome, she has to throw it into the fountain. Liliane is not sure she wants to return to Rome but, obediently, she throws the coin—a halfhearted toss that barely lands it in the water. More vivid in her mind is how a woman dressed in rags, holding a little girl with matted hair by the hand, follows her in the street and reaches up to touch the sleeve of Liliane's coat.

Signorina, the woman implores. *Per amore di dio, aiutar me*—for the love of God, help me.

Via! Liliane's father shouts at the woman, motioning with his hands. *Vattene!*—Go! Then, grabbing Liliane by the arm, he pulls her away from the beggar woman and the child.

"Gypsies! Thieves!" her father shouts.

Although not musical, her father has a gift for languages. He speaks German, French, English, and Spanish fluently. He picks up Italian in a few weeks. He also speaks a little Russian. His best friend, Tolia, is Russian.

It is not clear what Tolia does—he and Liliane's father make deals. Like Liliane's father, Tolia is divorced. His former wife is a well-known French journalist whose lover is an equally well-known journalist. Photographs of them vacationing together on a yacht on the Riviera or partying at an elegant country house often appear in *Paris Match*. Tolia is short and nearly bald, his eyes protrude, yet, for reasons unknown to Liliane, women like him. Is it his soulful look, which marks his Russian predilection for despair? His wry humor, which masks this Russian predilection for despair? Or his questionable past—a five-year prison term in Loos, near Lille, for fraud?

Liliane also likes Tolia. If, on occasion, he joins them for a meal she feels relief. So does her father. Tolia knows the latest gossip in Rome—who is sleeping with whom or, the reverse, who is no longer sleeping with whom—and although Liliane does not understand everything Tolia says, she understands enough. Next, Liliane's father teases Tolia about Véronique, a woman he was last seen with—Véronique will marry Gregory Peck. Tolia shrugs helplessly then, looking intently at Liliane with his soulful, protuberant eyes, he tells her father in uninflected but accented English: "You'll see, she is going to be a beauty," and although Liliane does not believe him, she blushes with pleasure.

Most evenings, Rudy dines at a restaurant called Nino. There are two restaurants called Nino in Rome, owned by two brothers. One brother is named Nino and his restaurant, located on Via Borgognona, is fashionable and expensive; the other brother is named Mario and his restaurant, located off Piazza Barberini, is less expensive. The Nino Rudy goes to is the one owned by Mario and since Rudy gave Mario a small part, the part of a restaurant owner, in one of his films (*Le Ragazze di Piazza di Spagna*), Mario is eager to please Rudy and, by extension, Liliane, for whom—in spite of Rudy's grudging approval—he makes a special pasta dish, rich with eggs and cheese. For Liliane's father, eating at Nino's comes closest to eating at home—or the idea of home. The atmosphere is cordial and lively. The diners shout to one another across the room, joking about the quality of the food, the slowness of the service. They know the waiters by name, long-suffering, sallow-looking men who, unperturbed, go about their business, ignoring the diners' impatient complaints and demands, part of an act in which the diners and the waiters are complicit. The food at Nino's is simple and good and, over the years, the waiters have remained the same.

Most nights, too, if he is not otherwise occupied, Rudy dines with Sergio Amidei. Sergio Amidei wrote the screenplays for most of Rudy's films; he also wrote many others, including those for Roberto Rossellini's *Rome, Open City,* and *Stromboli.* Like Rudy, Sergio Amidei is a bachelor. He always brings his bulldog, Cesare, to Nino's. Despite his thick leather collar studded with spikes, Cesare is old and gentle and every night he is fed a sumptuous dish of pasta in the kitchen. Often one or more friends of Rudy or of Sergio Amidei join them at their table. One evening, Anna Magnani dines with them and Liliane is shocked to see Anna Magnani chew with her mouth open and speak with her mouth full of food.

By far Liliane's favorite of her father's films is *Le Ragazze di Piazza di Spagna* (released in English as *Three Girls from Rome*). The film opens with a group of tourists—one of whom is played by Rudy—getting off a bus in front of the Spanish Steps. Assuredly leading the way, Rudy and the other tourists enter an eighteenth-century residence that has been converted into a museum, where the twenty-five-year-old Keats died of tuberculosis on February 23, 1821. The museum contains a large collection of paintings, letters, and manuscripts that pertain to Keats and Shelley as well as to Byron, Wordsworth, Elizabeth and Robert Browning, and Oscar Wilde. The memorabilia includes a lock of Keats's hair, Keats's death mask, and fragments of Shelley's bones. The film then moves on to the curator of the museum, played by Giorgio Bassani (the author of *The Garden of the Finzi-Continis*). From his office window, he observes three pretty girls who regularly come and sit on the Spanish Steps to have their lunch, and he narrates their stories.

One of the reasons Liliane likes the film is that she watches it being shot. Standing behind the big klieg lights—the film is shot on location—she watches how Lucia Bosé, Cosetta Grego, and Liliana Bonfatti sit together on a parapet on the Spanish Steps, their shapely legs dangling in the air while the makeup lady runs back and forth in between takes to comb their hair, apply more lipstick, or rearrange the folds of their clothes. In fairly straightforward and predictable fashion, the film follows the troubled romances of the three young women, seamstresses in a fashion house located on Piazza di Spagna. The tough, street-smart Liliana Bonfatti falls in love with a jockey, despite his short stature; betrayed by her lover, Cosetta Greco meets a kind taxi driver played by Marcello Mastroianni—in one of his

first big roles—and, in turn, they fall in love; Lucia Bosé plays a young woman who has moved up in the world from seamstress to fashion model, the source of friction and drama between her and her handsome boyfriend, a truck driver, played by Renato Salvatori. But, mainly, Liliane loves the film on account of Lucia Bosé. She is enchanted by her grace and beauty and wishes she could grow up to look like her. (Later Lucia Bosé will give up her acting career to marry the Spanish bullfighter Luis Miguel Domínguín.)

For this, her first Christmas in Rome, Liliane's father gives her a dress. Made of fine Italian cotton, the dress has smocking on the front and puffy sleeves and is babyish. To please her father, Liliane wears the dress on Christmas Day, but vows never to wear it again. Instead of packing it in her suitcase when she is getting ready to leave Rome, she shoves the dress out of sight underneath the white armoire. Cleaning, one day, she guesses, Maria will find it.

Mice find the dress and build a nest in it.

Liliane gives her father the key chain with the four-leaf clover charm she stole from the souvenir shop at the Shannon Airport. She is glad to be rid of it.

"For your car keys," she tells him. "Good luck," she adds.

Her father already owns a key chain for the silver Lancia— an elegant one with an Indian head eagle ten-dollar gold piece, designed by the sculptor Augustus Saint-Gaudens—and he is not superstitious. Nor is he religious. As far as Liliane knows, he does not pray or believe in luck or God.

II

Except for Liliane's mother who calls her *Liliane*—she also calls her *ma chérie*, my darling, or *ma petite chérie*, my little darling— and who speaks English with an indeterminate European accent, which could be German, French, or even Scandinavian (she is incapable of pronouncing a *j*, it comes out sounding like a *y*—*yelly, yunior*)—no one—not Liliane's new stepfather, not her teachers, nor her school friends—can pronounce her name the French way, the prettier way. They call her *Lillian* or *LilyAnne* or, worse, *Lil*.

On the other hand, Liliane's mother, Irène, insists that everyone pronounce her own name correctly: *Ee-wren* and not the American way, *Irene*. And everyone—including her second husband, who speaks only English—does. Born in Berlin—she does not like to give out the year—Irène is the youngest of three sisters. The sisters are lovely but, of the three, Irène is the loveliest.

Ursula, the oldest sister, is the free spirit. At seventeen, she runs away from home and marries a German officer, whom she divorces to marry an Englishman, whom she also divorces to marry a third time.

I love you, I love you not, I love you, I love you not, I love you. . . .

Ursula, known always as Uli, goes to live on a sisal estate in Tanganyika (present-day Tanzania), a British mandate under the League of Nations, with her third husband. She wants to be a writer and she does in fact write occasional columns for the local Dar es Salaam newspaper. She also begins but does not finish several children's books. But, in Africa, most of her time and energy is spent dealing with the household servants, who are numerous and often unreliable, learning to speak Swahili, and supervising the running of the school and local clinic on the estate; afterward, if she has time, she is driven a dozen or so miles on an unpaved road to the whites-only country club to play tennis and bridge—games she is good at and passionate about—and relax with a few, often a few too many, gin and tonics. She is also fond of animals and, over the years, she has had dogs, cats, a donkey, a mongoose, and a bushbuck as pets—the last the subject of one of the children's books. Snakes, too, are plentiful on the estate but not as welcome. Once, for several days, during breakfast, Uli, unsuspecting, sits on a nest of cobra eggs—the typical hatching time is between forty-eight and fifty days—that lies under her chair cushion on the veranda.

Mara ngapi nimekuambia . . . Uli scolds the two houseboys —How many times have I told you to shake out the cushions on the veranda each morning?

Embarrassed, the two houseboys laugh.

The next day, the two houseboys catch the cobra, chop off its head, and bury the head far away from the rest of the body; otherwise, they tell Uli, the head and body will join up at sunset and chase them.

Uli's third husband, Claus, is a descendant of a very old and aristocratic Baltic-German family that dates back to the twelfth century. His most colorful and reprehensible relative, Baron Roman Nikolai Maximilian von Ungern-Sternberg, also known as the Mad Baron of Mongolia, wrested control of Mongolia from the Chinese with his rogue band of Cossacks, Mongols, and Manchus and became a brutal warlord, persecuting both Russian Bolsheviks and Jews. Apparently, he devised the most horrific and cruel tortures for men, women, and children alike—there were beheadings, dismemberments, disembowelments, hangings from trees, tearing of limbs by wild animals, etc.—until he was taken prisoner by the Red Army and executed by a firing squad in 1921. As for Claus, Uli's husband, he is a courteous, mild-mannered man and prescient about his country's fate—during the Second World War, Estonia was occupied first by the Russians then by the Germans, then again by the Russians—and, in 1938, he decides to leave and go to Africa, where he finds work managing a sisal estate.

Located eighty miles south of Mombasa, near Tanga, a harbor on the East African coast, the 25,000-acre sisal estate Claus manages is owned by the London-based Ralli brothers: Zannis, Augustus, Zeus, Toumazis, and Eustratios, the original expatriate Greek merchants who amassed huge properties in the nineteenth century that extended all the way to Russia, India, and Africa. The sisal or agave plant resembles an overgrown pineapple and its rosette of sword-shaped leaves can grow up to two meters. The plant has a seven- to ten-year life span and will produce from 200 to 250 commercially viable leaves in its lifetime. By the mid-twentieth century, over 100,000 acres in East Africa are under sisal cultivation and produce over 200,000 tons of sisal. Sisal is the gold of Tanzania.

Thanks to her brief marriage to the Englishman, Uli is a British subject and since Claus emigrated from Estonia to East Africa as a "stateless" person, they are not interned, as most Germans are, during the Second World War. For their safety, they never speak German to each other, only English.

Jersey, knickers, boot, bloody, pudding, bollocks. . . .

According to a census taken in 1952, of the 17,885 Europeans living in Tanganyika, 12,395 or nearly 70 percent are British;

Greeks are the second largest group, followed by Italians (many of them former prisoners of war who elected to stay), then Dutch, German, Swiss, and American.

In the mid-1950s, Irène comes from America to visit Uli in Tanganyika. What a joy this is! The two sisters have not seen each other in how many years? Fifteen? Twenty? Not since before the war!

"You have not changed a bit," is how Uli greets Irène, whom she still calls by her childhood nickname—Rehlein, a diminutive meaning "little deer."

"Nor have you," Irène replies. Only she is not being truthful. Uli has aged. The African sun has hardened and darkened her skin, her blonde hair is streaked with gray, she has gained weight and walks with a pronounced limp—a problem with her hip.

"Still so beautiful," Uli continues. She cannot help admiring her youngest sister. "Your hair," she says, "and always so slim and elegant.

"But you must be tired after your long journey. Here, let me take you to your room," Uli also says, taking Irène by the arm.

The guest room on the sisal estate is very plain. The bed is covered with a local cotton bedspread that has a bright yellow and green pattern; over it hangs a mosquito net; a noisy electric fan dangles from the ceiling. The carpet in the bedroom is, of course, made out of sisal and hard on Irène's bare feet. There is a small wooden desk and next to it a wooden chair; the windows of the bedroom are shuttered and shut tight at night. Nonetheless, Irène has a hard time going to sleep, both on account of the time change and the strangeness of the place; and she can hear the night watchman shuffling outside as he makes his rounds guarding the house. The bathroom is far down the hall.

But Irène has spent nights in less comfortable rooms than this one. The one that comes to mind right away is the room in which she spent the night with Liliane's father, Rudy, at the camp in Marolles. Situated under the eaves of an inn, the room was filled with discarded furniture, trunks, rusty, broken tools. The bed consisted of a mattress on the floor; instead of sheets there was a stained quilt that smelled of a disinfectant. Despite her reservations, Irène had made an effort and wore a pink silk nightgown.

Irène takes several photographs during her stay on the sisal estate—snapshots. The ones of Uli sitting on the veranda—no doubt in the same chair that hid the cobra eggs—are blurry and out of focus, often her back is to the camera (perhaps Uli senses that she is no longer as pretty or as photogenic); a photo of Claus shows him wearing khaki shorts and a short-sleeve shirt and standing robustly in a field, pointing to the sisal plants. Perhaps he is explaining to Irène, his sister-in-law, how the fibers, called cordage, taken from the plant leaf and extracted by a process known as decortication, are used to make rope as well as carpets, low-cost paper, handicrafts, and—but is Irène listening to Claus? Is she interested in the sisal plants? But perhaps, too, Claus is flirting a little with her. In the photo, Claus looks to be a handsome man.

There are photos of Bibi, the nurse-midwife; Juma, the cook; Nyatta and Andrea, the houseboys; Pita, the gardener.

There is a sweet photo of the schoolchildren standing to attention in front of their desks, in honor, no doubt, of the blonde visitor from America; another photo shows half a dozen sisal workers standing behind a long wooden table, stripping or decorticating the sisal fibers that run along the length of the leaves.

As children the two sisters were not close—mostly on account of the difference in their ages (when Uli left home to marry the German officer, Irène was twelve). Now, in Africa, things between them are different, more equal. They can reminisce and laugh about their childhood: their lack of education (neither one finished high school); their passion for sports (they both played field hockey, they both were and still are avid tennis players); their moody, unhappy mother, Louise, who left them in the care of an indifferent governess each winter to go to the South of France; their stern father, Waldemar, a Prussian officer—but they do not reminisce or laugh about how, when they were little girls, he made them sit on his lap, bouncing them up and down to arouse himself.

Little Rehlein, pretty little deer—caught.

Safer to delve further back to their paternal grandfather, and Uli asks, "Didn't Opapa take out Kaiser Wilhelm's appendix?"

"Yes, then the Kaiser made Opapa grand ducal privy counselor and he became a famous doctor," Irène says.

"But what I remember best," Irène continues, "is the story our mother told us about how, one afternoon, she and her younger sister were playing in Sans Souci Park—the whole family had had to move from their home in Jena to Potsdam while the Kaiser was recuperating from the appendectomy in case something went wrong—and how he walked by and asked them if they were twins."

"Oh, I remember that story," Uli says with a laugh. "Our mother was so frightened at being addressed by the Kaiser that she said yes, although she and her sister weren't twins."

"And it is always easier to say yes," Irène adds.

Irène, the most reticent of the three sisters, has said yes often— too often—when, probably, she should have said no. She blames the war. She blames having been left on her own, having to fend for herself. And she was too young, she was too . . . she cannot think of the right words to express her indignation, her sense of injustice of what happened to her. Of being abandoned.

Her husband was gone. A prisoner, he was interned in a godforsaken village in the Loire Valley, soon to be sent back to either Germany or who-knows-where in North Africa. On her own for the first time in her life, she had to ask for help from people she did not particularly like or trust. She had to depend on their goodwill, on their advice. She had to rely on them for money. For papers. For gasoline for the car, so that she, too, could leave. And, nothing, she learned, came free.

She was courageous or, maybe, just naïve.

On a sunny spring day in May 1940, tired of waiting—waiting for the German troops to march into Belgium, into the Netherlands and Luxembourg—Irène packed up her husband's cream-colored convertible Packard with suitcases filled with clothes and valuables, several cans of gas she had hoarded, Liliane's porcelain chamber pot, and food (bread, cheese, sausage, oranges); and with Liliane, her seven-month-old daughter, and Jeanne, the nineteen-year-old nanny from Brittany, she drove south. As a precaution, to be less conspicuous on the road she tied a scarf around her blonde hair.

Irène was unaccustomed to driving long distances—the gear stick was stiff and hard to shift—and she had hired a young man from her husband's office to accompany her as far as Biarritz. His name was Jean-Pierre and he came in handy. Jean-Pierre took turns with Irène driving the Packard and he changed the flat tire they had en route. Although young, in his twenties, he helped shield Irène from the mocking remarks and lewd stares of the men they encountered along the way. For the time being, she had enough money, the necessary papers, the entry and exit visas, to drive to Portugal. Fortunately, too, Irène left a little ahead of the mass exodus—the first one, which began only ew weeks later, when the Germans finally invaded France, he second and much larger one, later in June, when the s entered Paris and four million people left the capital d south.

Irène does not like to think about the trip. In fact, she has almost blocked it out of her mind. But then, from time to time, like a bad dream, she remembers patches of dark road bordered by trees whose trunks are ringed in white paint, a field of sunflowers all facing in the same direction, toward the sun, a shutter banging against the house all night in her shabby hotel room. During the entire journey, Liliane cries—a high-pitched animal wail. Nothing Jeanne does can console her. Later, it turns out—the thermometer forgotten in Paris—Liliane had a fever of 40 degrees Celsius.

In New York City, where she now lives with her second husband, Irène's apartment is large and comfortable. Three bedrooms, two bathrooms, a library, a large living room, dining room, kitchen and pantry, two maid's rooms—all furnished with English antiques and pretty chintzes, all in good taste. She also has help—a live-in cook, Helena, who is Finnish and, on occasion, drinks too much, and a cleaning lady, Brigid, who is Irish and who comes three times a week and does the laundry and the ironing. (The two women do not get along but their quarrels do not interest Irène and she ignores their complaints.)

Two mornings a week, Irène goes to an exercise studio. The studio—not a gym—is run by Nicholas Kounovsky, a charismatic Russian from Odessa, who devised a series of European-style fitness exercises based on six elements he calls "sixometry": endurance, suppleness, balance, strength, speed, and coordination. Irène, naturally athletic and coordinated, quickly becomes adept at doing the exercises and can effortlessly raise herself up on the rings and hang upside down by her knees on the trapeze.

One day a week, Irène goes to another studio. She has taken up oil painting. Her paintings are, for the most part, abstract, messy splashes of colors—green, orange, yellow, colors Irène admits she does not like—and are thickly layered, too bright and rushed. Edgar, the owner and master of the painting studio, makes an occasional remark about how Irène is expressing her unconscious or subconscious feelings—he does not differentiate between the two—and he encourages Irène.

"You should come to the studio more often," Edgar tells her. "Once a week is not enough. You have talent. Trust me. I know. You have to work harder. Make it count. Make it your life."

But Irène does not want to make painting her life. Her life, she thinks, is filled up enough with her new country, a new husband, and, of course, Liliane.

If, from time to time, Irène brings one of her paintings home from the studio to the apartment, the painting does not fit in with the chintzes and English antiques and she ends up putting the painting away in a closet.

Irène's new American husband, Gaby, is not as encouraging as Edgar, the owner of the studio. He does not much like Irène's paintings or, more accurately, he does not understand them. He is accustomed to representational artwork—ancestral portraits, familiar landscapes, still lifes. As a result, he does not know what to say about Irène's paintings, except to say that he is glad that they keep her occupied.

Gaby has never been married before. Gaby has never met vone like Irène before. To him, she is both glamorous and mys-
ıs. Exotic, he might say. A German-French divorcée, with a
d with an eight-year-old child. Gaby is conservative, as is

his family. Good Episcopalian Republicans from New England who can trace their ancestors back to the Pilgrim Fathers and who make no bones about being disapproving. About being bigoted. Among themselves they whisper: A German? A woman once married to a Jew? And what about the child with the unpronounceable name? Nothing good can come of it.

Gaby does not know what to make of the child either. For one thing, she speaks Spanish and French and has not yet learned English. She is a bit overweight in a pale, unhealthy, or, more likely, a badly nourished sort of way; she has straight brown hair and does not look like her mother.

Lillian—he calls her.

Liliane looks a little like Barbara, the middle sister, a brunette. Barbara is a doctor. A dermatologist. Married briefly and divorced, Barbara is kind and even-tempered. Like Irène, she will come and live in America. Only she will come to America several years later, in the mid-fifties, under different circumstances— with little money and no marriage prospects—and Gaby has to sponsor her and sign an affidavit that Barbara will not become a public charge. Once in New York, Barbara rents a small apartment in Queens. Before she can practice medicine again, she has to go back to school and take refresher courses—the United States does not recognize her German medical degree because she obtained it in 1945, when the Germans were thought to have rushed medical students through school in order to have enough doctors for the war effort. Poor Barbara, at first, she has a rough time of it: at her age—she is nearly forty—she has to work as an intern in a hospital, she does not have much money, and she has to relearn everything in English. The good news is that everyone, right away, likes Barbara. Everyone except, perhaps, Irène.

Irène does not dislike her sister but her sister irritates her. Liliane hears them arguing in the library.

"How can you go out with him?" Irène says. "He's a Nazi."

"How can you say he's a Nazi when he's Jewish?"

"He's German," Irène says. "I don't want German friends. And he's a dwarf."

"You're such a snob, Rehlein," Barbara says, laughing. "He's not a dwarf, he's just short."

"And I wish you would wear something a little nicer when you come here for dinner," Irène says to change the subject. "What will Gaby think?"

"What's wrong with my skirt? What's wrong with my sweater?" Barbara asks. "They're perfectly fine. And I don't think Gaby will care."

"Well, I care how you look," Irène says. "And what happened to all the clothes I gave you?"

"I have them," Barbara says.

"Well, why don't you wear them," Irène says sharply.

Irène and Barbara rarely speak German together. They rarely reminisce about how as children they lived in a large, sunny apartment in the Charlottenburg district of Berlin and how, from the balcony of the apartment, they could look down on the manicured lawn and ornate flower beds of Karolinger Platz. It would be pointless. Or too painful. Barbara was there when, in 1942, the apartment building on Karolinger Platz was bombed in an Allied air raid. She watched everything burn to the ground. Nothing was left of her family's belongings—not a scrap of cloth, not a dish, not a single photograph.

Soon after, Barbara and her parents, Waldemar and Louise, left Berlin. They went to live in Austria, where they owned a summer chalet.

Liliane remembers the chalet; she and her mother went to visit Louise in Innsbruck immediately after the war. By then, Louise was living alone. Waldemar, a heavy smoker—so addicted that during the war, when cigarettes were scarce, he picked butts off the street—had died a few years earlier of lung cancer. Louise, too, was nearly dead, from malnourishment—she weighed eighty pounds. The chalet was requisitioned during the war and each room was occupied by a family of refugees. As the owner, Louise was allowed to choose a single room and, wisely, she chose the kitchen. On account of the stove, it was the warmest.

Up a steep hill banked with flowering bushes, the wooden chalet with its balconies and peaked roof looked like a storybook chalet. Liliane half expected to find Heidi and her grandfather, surrounded by friendly goats, inhabiting it. The outside of the chalet was pretty and bucolic but the inside was quite different. The refugee families had recently left and left a mess—broken furniture, mattresses with the stuffing coming out, torn curtains, broken dishes, and bottles littered the floor. Louise was making preparations to leave as well, and go to Nice. Frail, worn out, depressed, she wanted to live in the sun.

*   *   *

What Liliane also remembers about Innsbruck is the amputees. Nearly all the men in the city were missing an arm, a leg, or both legs. They hobbled on crutches or walked leaning on canes, their empty sleeves or pant legs, neatly pinned up, useless reminders. A main transport hub, where four important rail lines converged, Innsbruck was also a railroad supply center for Italy and a strategic target in 1943. For two years, the city was heavily bombed. By the time the war ended, the railroad yards and 60 percent of the buildings in Innsbruck—the seventeenth-century Servitenkloster monastery; the Bartholomäiskapelle, one of the oldest buildings in Innsbruck; the Landhaus, or federal state parliament, built in 1724; the city hall; St. James's Cathedral; and the Jesuit Church (fortunately, the crypt that houses the tomb of Archduke Leopold V of Austria and his wife, Claudia of Medici, the founders of the church, survived the bombing)—were either destroyed or badly damaged.

During the war, Barbara studies for her medical degree in Innsbruck. More than once, she watches as the Allied planes, their metal bodies glistening in the sun, drop their load of bombs on the city; she can see how the bombs fall and how, when they hit the ground, they explode and, like leaves in the wind, everything blows up in the air. The first time, the Allies were aiming for the bridges across the Inn River; instead they hit the houses along the riverbanks. As yet, there were no air raid shelters in Innsbruck and 265 people were either injured or killed. Barbara saw many of them—both those who were brought to the hospital in time as well as those who were not.

The first Allied troops to arrive in Innsbruck after the war are the Americans. How Barbara makes friends with them Liliane guesses—

Late one night, a jeep drives up and brakes abruptly at the emergency entrance of the Innsbruck hospital. Two soldiers jump out, carrying a third soldier who is unconscious and bleeding.

The soldiers have been drinking. On their way back to the barracks, one of them fell, impaling himself on the spike of a metal railing. Once inside the hospital, a soldier shouts, "Emergency! We need a doctor, right now!"

A dark-haired young woman, dressed in a white coat, who has been asleep at her station—her head resting on the desk—quickly rouses herself.

"Yes, I'm a doctor," she tells them in a heavily accented English.

The American soldiers bring Barbara food—chocolate, coffee, butter, dried eggs, tinned ham—which she shares with poor, undernourished Louise. They bring her cigarettes and whiskey, too, which Barbara does not share with her mother. Instead, for the first time since before the war, she has fun, she relaxes. She drinks, smokes, and dances with the American soldiers; she even falls in love with one or two of them. Why not? She has not had sex in a long time. Before they leave, the American soldiers promise not to forget her. They promise to help her.

At long last, Barbara receives her medical degree in America and she is allowed to practice dermatology in the state of Rhode Island. She rents a modest apartment in Newport—a bedroom, living room, and kitchenette (Barbara rarely cooks and, more often than not, she eats her dinner standing up, straight out of the can)—with an adjoining office on the ground floor of a private house on Touro Street. Touro Street is a few blocks from the harbor and, after work, in the summer, Barbara likes to walk down among the tourists and look at the boats, then go and sit in a café and order a glass of chardonnay. Always friendly and curious, she often starts up a conversation with a stranger at the next table.

"Where are you from?" the stranger may ask. "I mean because of your accent."

"Germany."

"My brother was stationed in Germany right after the war," the stranger volunteers. "He was with the Twelfth Armored Division and I still remember some of the pictures he took while he was over there. There was one of a whole bunch of German prisoners being marched down the street, their hands up in the air, a lot of them are smiling and laughing as if relieved—relieved the war is over and relieved to be alive, I suppose. I am trying to remember the name of the city he was in—it was on the Danube."

"Dillingen," Barbara says.

"Yes, that's it! Dillingen! How did you know?"

"After the war, I worked there as a doctor, in Luitpold, a displaced persons camp."

"You're a doctor? So am I," the stranger says.

"Small world," the stranger adds.

On summer weekends, in Newport, Barbara goes to the beach and swims. She is a strong swimmer and not afraid to swim far out. Depending on the weather, she swims long after Labor Day

and after the tourists have gone home, and she swims alone. Once, from Bailey's Beach, Barbara was nearly swept out to sea by a riptide. When she mentioned it, she made light of it.

"The important thing is not to panic and to keep swimming parallel to the shore until you get free of the current."

"You could have drowned," Liliane says.

Barbara works hard at her medical practice and, over the years, acquires a lot of patients—some of whom are rich and have well-known names—and an excellent reputation. One day her secretary gets a call from the White House. The person on the phone from the White House wants to know whether Barbara will fly down to Washington to take a look at the blemishes on the First Lady's face. Of course Barbara will. The blemishes turn out not to be serious—the First Lady is not using a proper cleanser. Barbara has been told to be discreet about her visit. She is—for the most part—but she cannot resist telling her sister Irène.

"What did you charge Jackie?" Irène wants to know.

"What I always charge," Barbara answers. "Twenty-five dollars."

Liliane loves this story. An American success story.

Liliane is especially fond of Aunt Barbara. Although she is no fonder of Barbara than she is of her own mother, she is fond of her in a different way. Partly because Barbara is a doctor, which grants her special knowledge, but mostly because Barbara is interested in what Liliane has to say or what she thinks.

For instance, Liliane tells Barbara what she, as yet, has not told anyone: "I think I want to become a writer."

Or, what is also a great deal on Liliane's mind at the time: "If I sleep with someone for the first time, how can I make sure not to get pregnant?"

Like Uli and Irène, Barbara married very young—at nineteen. She married a man who was twelve years older and who shared none of her interests. Soon after, like Uli and Irène, Barbara got divorced, but unlike Uli and Irène, she does not remarry.

"Did you have to get married?" Liliane asks her.

"No."

"Were you in love then?"

"No. Not really."

"Then why?" Liliane insists.

"I wanted to leave. Leave home."

"Why?" Liliane asks again.

But it is one of the things Barbara does not want to talk about.

"The same reason your mother left home," Barbara answers.

"Ask her. Ask Rehlein," she also says.

III

In July 1940, Irène, Liliane, and Jeanne, the young nanny from Brittany, set sail from Lisbon to New York on board the SS *Exeter*. The SS *Exeter*, the SS *Excalibur*, the SS *Excambion*, and the SS *Exochorda* are nearly identical ocean liners known as the "Four Aces." Built in the early 1930s by American Export Lines, the ships were considered the ultimate in comfort as they plied their way back and forth across the Atlantic and the Mediterranean. Each had superbly furnished staterooms with private bathrooms, elegant lounges with painted woodwork, a Smoke Room Bar upholstered in green leather, and dining rooms set with the finest crystal and bone china. But when the war breaks out in Europe, these luxurious cruises come to an abrupt halt and, instead, the SS *Exeter* and the SS *Excalibur* make several risky round-trip voyages—by 1940, the Atlantic is heavily mined—between Portugal and the United States, transporting thousands of refugees to safety. Once the United States enters the war, the

"Four Aces" are appropriated by the U.S. Navy and converted into troopships. The SS *Excalibur* is renamed the USS *Joseph Hewes* and is torpedoed by a German submarine in 1942; in the same year, the SS *Exeter,* renamed the USS *Edward Rutledge,* is also torpedoed and sinks off the coast of Casablanca; in 1943, the SS *Excambion,* renamed the USS *John Penn,* is sunk by a Japanese torpedo bomber off Guadalcanal; only the SS *Exochorda,* renamed the USS *Harry Lee,* survives the war.

Irène has had to leave behind almost all her belongings— her beautiful Patou suits, her Revillon furs—in the apartment on Rue Raynouard, as well as the silver, the china, the paintings, and Liliane's elegant midnight navy Silver Cross pram which, in any case, Liliane will have outgrown. A photo taken on the deck of the SS *Exeter* shows Irène leaning against the ship's railing, looking tan and fit. She is wearing white shorts, and, on her head, tilted at a jaunty angle, she wears the ship captain's cap. In another photo, Irène, who loves to sunbathe, is stretched out on a deck chair wearing a two-piece bathing suit. In a third photo,

still in her two-piece bathing suit, Irène is holding Liliane on her lap. In all these photos, Irène is smiling—there is no sign of anxiety or worry on her lovely face. In mid-Atlantic, can the war already be so far behind and forgotten? There are a few photos of fellow passengers—nameless women and children—most likely refugees like Irène and Liliane. And, finally, a photo of the captain himself, who has recovered his cap and is smiling. There are no photos of Jeanne.

Jeanne is pale, plain, nearsighted. She comes from a small town on the Atlantic coast of Brittany, once famous for its sardine fishing and canning industries; a town with a nearly unpronounceable name—Douarnenez. Jeanne will devote five years of her life—her young life—to taking care of Liliane. Five years she will spend in Peru.

Peru of all places.

What was she thinking?

Jeanne, we have to leave Paris. Leave France, is what Irène says to her.

You'll have to get a passport. A visa.

Oui, madame.

Does she have a choice?

Might she have said, *Non, madame, I have to go back to my home, to my family?*

The men in Jeanne's family are fishermen, the women are robust, hardworking, and uncomplaining. Except for her parents, who spent their honeymoon on Mont Saint-Michel, none of her family has ever been farther away from home than the city of Brest. As far as they are concerned, Jeanne has disappeared off the face of the earth.

Pérou, where in God's name is that? Jeanne's father, a large man with an appetite for food and life, might well ask his wife, Jeanne's mother. But he has to look it up for himself in one of the children's school atlases. He shakes his head sadly; in his heart, he knows he will not see Jeanne again.

Pérou, Annick, Jeanne's younger sister and the prettiest, says with a huge sigh. *How I envy her. I would do anything to get away from this stupid place.* And, in a few months' time, on a warm summer morning, wearing her best dress, a sleeveless, red-and-white flower print, and bicycling quickly, without giving the village a second glance, she does just that.

Jeanne does not speak Spanish. How will she manage? Handsome, curly-haired Daniel, the cleverest of Jeanne's brothers, asks.

Is she so attached to the child that she cannot be parted from her? wonders Catherine, a schoolteacher, and Jeanne's favorite sister.

More than likely, a simple girl, Jeanne feels it is her duty. And, a Catholic, she is deeply religious.

Or, perhaps, she has misunderstood—misunderstood the way everyone else has at the time.

The British call it the Phoney War.

The French, *la drôle de guerre*.

Those terms refer to the six-month period, from October 1939 through March 1940, that followed the German occupation of Poland, after war had been declared between Germany and the Allies but when no armed hostilities take place. Already, however, German submarines have torpedoed several British ships, including the HMS *Courageous* with a loss of 518 men, the HMS *Royal Oak* with an even greater loss of 833 men, and the SS *Athenia*, a passenger liner, on its way from Glasgow to Montreal, causing the loss of 117 lives. One of those lost lives belonged to a ten-year-old Canadian girl named Margaret Hayworth. Her death was widely publicized in the newspapers and became a rallying war cry. A thousand people met the train that transported Margaret's body back to Ontario and her funeral was attended by many Canadian government officials as well as by the entire Ontario cabinet.

Irène, Liliane, and Jeanne spend three days in the United States— in Riverdale, New York—with friends of Rudy. Rudy's friends take Irène to the World's Fair and Irène can't help but notice how carefree and prosperous everyone looks. The most memorable exhibit was the Futurama ride sponsored by General Motors, which carried Irène past an American utopian landscape that focused on transportation, roadways, and modernist buildings while a narrator described the world of tomorrow—the year 1960. But by far Irène's favorite exhibit is the Aquacade—the lights, the waterfalls, the hundreds of nearly identical beautiful girls diving and swimming in perfect sync.

Jeanne takes Liliane for walks in a borrowed stroller past well-tended gardens and large, expensive-looking houses. Rudy's friends' house is large as well and has a solarium filled with exotic plants and a built-in basin filled with orange carp. Liliane is fascinated by the carp and, holding on to the rim of the basin to stand—she has just learned how—she watches the carp for hours at a time.

On the third day, Rudy's friends drive Irène, Liliane, and Jeanne to the airport, and they fly to Miami. From Miami, they fly to Lima, Peru.

Panagra, short for Pan American–Grace Airways, was the first U.S. airline carrier to schedule passenger, mail and freight flights across the equator and link the west coast of South America to the east coast across the Andes, the highest mountain range in the Americas. From the late 1920s to the mid-1960s, Panagra planes were such a regular presence in the skies that to even the remotest tribes in the jungles of Ecuador and Peru, the word "panagra" meant "high." At the time all trans-Andean flights were made under visual conditions; route maps and aeronautical charts were primitive at best, and the pilots had to be able to recognize geographic landmarks over which they were flying—mountain peaks, rivers, lakes. One Panagra pilot, according to popular legend, when repeatedly asked by a radio operator for his position, answered crossly, "Tell them we are east of the moon and slightly under it." The plane, a DC-3, Irène, Liliane, and Jeanne are on tosses and bucks its way over the Andes so violently that most of the passengers are sick. Jeanne, who has only flown once before from New York to Miami, is sick as well. Irène, too, is afraid that she is going to throw up—the smell in the cabin is enough to make anyone vomit—but she is holding Liliane on her lap and that distracts her. Luckily, Liliane is asleep. Once the plane has crossed the Andes and is out of the turbulence, the pilot, a tall, blond American with a crew cut, walks down the aisle to check on the passengers. He stops to talk to Irène.

"Sorry about that," he tells her. "Air pockets," he explains.

"Where are you folks from?" he continues.

Irène tells him.

"Are you getting off in Lima?"

Perched on Irène's armrest, the pilot takes out a pad and pencil from his pocket and writes addresses down. "I'll be seeing

you," he also says, patting Irène's arm, before he gets up and goes back to the cockpit.

Lima, a city Irène has barely heard of; a city where it never rains; a city where it is always hot, exceedingly hot; a city where she does not speak the language and where she knows no one—including her husband's relatives, whom she has yet to meet—and a city where there are frequent earthquakes. A few weeks earlier a powerful earthquake—8.2 on the Richter scale—caused massive damage to the city, nearly destroying the Cathedral of Lima, and killing and injuring more than three thousand people. Most of the earthquakes occur in the middle of the night and Jeanne will have to quickly get out of bed with just enough time to find and put on her glasses but not enough time to find and put on her robe, then run into Liliane's room and wake her so that, together, they can go stand in the doorway of the bedroom, said to be the safest place in the house.

The rented house is in the upscale Miraflores district of Lima. The house has a large garden surrounded by a high stone wall, topped with shards of broken glass to keep out thieves. The servants—the cook, the maid, the part-time gardener and chauffeur, Mañuel—talk constantly about how, at night, all the thieves need do is climb over the garden wall to rob the houses of the rich. They give examples: only two weeks ago, the Martinez house, down the street, the cook says, pointing a greasy finger, was robbed. All the jewelry, all the silverware was taken. Another house, the house directly in back of us, Mañuel says, while the Gomez family was out for only a few hours at the movies, was robbed. Of everything—the furniture, the paintings, the curtains. *Toto*—everything.

Liliane's mother and her friends talk about how unreliable the servants are and how they are certain that the servants are robbing them.

Liliane is more afraid of thieves than she is of earthquakes.

"Jeanne!" she calls out in the middle of the night. She is having a nightmare. And Jeanne comes running into her room.

Taking Liliane in her arms, Jeanne rocks her until she is comforted and calm. It is then, too, in the darkened room, that Jeanne tells Liliane about her family in Brittany.

"Tell me again about Annick," Liliane begs her.

"Oh, Annick, she is the naughty one . . ." Jeanne begins.

Soon after Jeanne leaves, Annick bicycles the twenty-five kilometers to Quimper and, leaving her bicycle at the train station, she buys a third-class ticket to Paris. Once in Paris, she walks aimlessly from the Gare Montparnasse down Rue de Vaugirard. It is late and she is tired and hungry. Eventually, she finds a café that is open and goes inside. She orders coffee and a ham sandwich. At this hour, the café is not very crowded—in fact, it is about to close—and since the bartender who is also the proprietor of the café does not have much to do, he watches Annick as she eats her sandwich. She is very pretty and he has a special fondness for redheads.

Annick, when she has finished eating her sandwich and drinking her coffee and is ready to pay for her meal, summons up her courage to ask the bartender —she cannot help noticing that he has been looking at her—whether he needs help in his café. She can waitress, she tells him. The bartender seems to give it some thought and lights a cigarette.

He also offers Annick a cigarette and she takes one, although she does not yet smoke.

Lighting her cigarette, the bartender smiles and asks Annick where she is from.

Blowing out smoke without inhaling it, Annick tells him. She also explains how she felt as if she would suffocate in Douarnenez—I could not breathe, she tells the bartender, fanning her face with her free hand, and she had to leave.

The bartender says he understands; he, too, comes from a small village, in Burgundy, and left when he was sixteen years old. Village life is not very amusing, he says, while life in Paris is.

He then says that he would like to help Annick and, if she can, as she says, wait on tables, wash up, and serve drinks, he will hire her on a trial basis.

Does she have a place to stay? He asks her.

Not yet, Annick answers. She has saved a little money and she is planning on finding a cheap hotel.

The bartender says he has a better idea.

"And tell me about Daniel." Liliane likes Daniel.

"Oh, Daniel," Jeanne says, "Daniel is the clever one and you should see how handsome he is. For miles around Douarnenez, all the girls are in love with Daniel."

Jeanne kisses Liliane, once, twice on the cheek, before she falls asleep.

Most of the time, Jeanne is not affectionate. She is a disciplinarian. Rarely does Liliane disobey her. If she tries to play a trick or fool Jeanne in a silly way, Jeanne is not amused. For instance, once, while they are taking a walk, Liliane sees a dog turd lying on the ground, brown, fresh, perfectly formed and still steaming. "Look," she tells Jeanne, pointing, *"une saucisse"*—a sausage, and, stretching down her hand, Liliane makes as if to pick it up. Yanking her hard by the arm—so hard, she leaves a red mark—Jeanne threatens to tell Liliane's mother.

Liliane's mother is out a great deal. She has joined the Lima Country Club and has made friends—Peruvian as well as American friends. During the day, she swims, plays tennis and golf; in the evening, she plays bridge, then she goes out to dinner. Mañuel, the chauffeur, drives her to the club in the morning and picks her up later in the afternoon. In the evening, Irène makes other arrangements—Liliane often overhears the maid announce that Señor Jerry, the American Panagra pilot, is waiting downstairs for her or, at other times, that a Señor Diego is downstairs.

Occasionally, Irène brings Liliane to the Lima Country Club pool. If Jerry is not flying a plane, he is swimming laps or doing perfect jackknives from the high diving board.

Drink trays in hand, the Peruvian waiters stop to watch him.

"*Mira a ese hombre!*"—Look at that man! one of them says.

"Come on in," Jerry calls out to Liliane's mother.

Adjusting the straps to her two-piece suit and putting on her bathing cap, Irène stands up and dives neatly into the pool, but just before she hits the water, her feet cross. When she surfaces, Jerry splashes water at her and, laughing, Irène splashes back, then, disappearing, Jerry dives down in the pool, which makes Irène yelp and swim away. Resurfacing and shouting something that Liliane does not understand, Jerry catches up with Irène and they both go under. They remain underwater for such a long time that Liliane wonders if they have drowned.

When, at last, Irène and Jerry come up for air, they let out their breaths in noisy gasps, spit water, and laugh.

Irène is in her early twenties. Until now, in Peru, she has never had fun. Life growing up in the apartment on Karolinger Platz in Berlin was, at best, somber. Her father, Waldemar, is a stern, humorless, unapproachable presence, except, when, in the evening, after he has had a few drinks, he tries to cajole little Rehlein to sit on his lap. Listless and depressed, Irène's mother, Louise, often stays in bed all day, complaining of a migraine. She cannot tolerate the slightest noise in the apartment—a door shutting, a toilet flushing down the hall—and Irène and her sisters have to tiptoe from room to room and speak in whispers. And, as sometimes happens, should Barbara forget and laugh too loudly or should Uli drop her books on the dining room table, invariably, their governess or, if he is at home, their father—as if each has been waiting for just such an infraction—angrily shouts: *Ruhe!*—Quiet!

One time, Louise takes too many sleeping pills—it is never clear whether she does so on purpose—and the doctor who is called in has to pump out her stomach. Irène, who is fifteen at the time and the only daughter still at home, is made to assist the doctor. She watches as he quickly, almost callously, strips Louise of her nightgown—Irène has never seen her mother naked and the sight of her small, limp breasts and the indecent amount of curly light brown pubic hair that spreads nearly to Louise's belly button embarrasses her. She watches as the doctor inserts a tube in Louise's mouth and works it down to her stomach—he has to be careful, he observes almost offhandedly, not to insert it into her lungs—and as he administers small amounts of warm saline solution into the tube, which he then siphons back up into the basin that Irène is holding. Irène's hands tremble so violently that the water sloshes back and forth ready to spill out. Fortunately, Louise is unconscious during the procedure.

Life in Paris is only a slight improvement for Irène: she has to learn to speak French and she has to behave like an adult and a wife—look after the apartment on Rue Raynouard, plan menus, entertain. Also—although she does not like to admit this—she is a bit afraid of Rudy and his indifference to household matters unnerves her. "Do what you like," he tells her whenever Irène asks for his advice about, for instance, a dinner menu or what clothes to wear. "Do what you think is best." And, although generous—he buys her the Revillon fur coat, the Patou suits, a gold Cartier pin with rubies in the shape of a bird—most of Rudy's attention is on his work, on his deals, and Irène is lonely. When she becomes pregnant, much of the nine months she feels sick—so sick that once, after lunch at Fouquet's, she throws up on the Champs-Élysées.

Jerry tries to coax Liliane into the pool with him—by then she is nearly four years old.—Time you learned how to swim, he tells her and, without waiting for an answer, he picks her up. Jerry's body feels lean and warm and Liliane wraps her arms tightly around his neck.

"Kick," Jerry says as he lowers Liliane into the water. He has forgotten that Liliane does not speak English. "*Patear con las piernas*"—Kick with your legs, he repeats in Spanish, motioning with his hands.

"Thatta girl," Jerry says, although Liliane has begun to sink in the water and he has to grab her and bring her back to the surface.

When Irène receives a letter in Lima from Rudy, the letter is dated weeks earlier and heavily censored—entire lines are crossed out in black ink. Irène has difficulty reading it and she can never make out where he is or whether he can get the necessary papers—at present, he still has no passport—to join them in South America.

Je t'aime—I love you, he writes to Irène.

Embrasses Liliane de ma part—Kiss Liliane for me, he writes.

Only a few months old when she saw her father, Liliane does not remember him. In her mother's bedroom in the house in Miraflores there is a framed photo of him on the bureau. In the photo, Rudy, unsmiling, is looking straight into the camera; his hands are in his pockets and he is wearing his Foreign Legionnaire's uniform: a dark jacket, dark jodhpurlike pants and puttees. The harder Liliane looks at the photograph, the less familiar Rudy becomes.

On her mother's bedside table, in a silver frame, there is another photo. In it, Irène and Rudy are smiling and walking arm in arm in the snow; they are wearing knickers and Irène is holding a little white dog on a leash.

"We were in Saint-Moritz," Irène tells Liliane.

"Oh, Hansi! He's so cute," picking up the photo, Liliane exclaims about the dog. "What happened to him?"

"We had to leave him. Leave him with the concierge in Paris. She promised to take good care of him."

"I want a dog," Liliane says. "Can I have a dog?" she repeats.

"Careful," Irène tells Liliane. "The frame is silver."

*   *   *

From time to time, Irène leaves Lima for a few days to go to a beach resort with her friends. One time, she is gone for a week on a trip to Cuzco and Machu Picchu. There are more photographs: Irène on horseback, sitting uncomfortably in the saddle—she is afraid of horses; a photo of a young boy wearing a poncho and a knitted cap; someone—perhaps Irène—bathing in a hot spring; a photo of a bunch of vicuñas; a photo showing the train that goes from Cuzco to Machu Picchu; a photo of the Urubamba River and the Sacred Valley; three photos of the ruins of Machu Picchu covered by a low cloud bank, with a sharp peak rising through the clouds in the distance.

It is hard to tell from the photos whether Irène is having a good time on the trip. Is she interested in the ancient civilization? Does she think it a mystical site?

"Follow me, señor, and I will show you the palace of Inti, the Sun God" is what the eleven-year-old Quechua boy, Pablito Alvarez, told Hiram Bingham as he led him up the steep canyon to discover the Machu Picchu ruins in 1911.

"No one knows for certain whether Machu Picchu was built as a symbol of Inca power or whether it was built as a sacred place," the guide is saying.

Standing at the site of the sacred pillar aligned with the four highest Andean peaks, Irène, on account of the cloud bank, can only see one of them.

"The *intihuatana* stone," the guide continues tonelessly and by rote, pointing to the pillar, "is the precise indicator of the equinoxes. At midday, on March 21 and on September 21, the sun stands at the top of the pillar and casts no shadow. The Incas observed this and tried to stop the progress of the sun by holding ceremonies on those days."

The guide adds, "Sacrificial ceremonies."

"What sort of sacrifices?" Irène asks.

"Virgins. Virgins of the Sun, as the young girls chosen to serve the Inca emperor were called. Most of the skeletons found in Machu Picchu were small and of women, which shows that—"

"Nonsense," Diego interrupts. "The Inca people are small—small-boned."

The guide says nothing.

"The skeletons belonged to the emperor's servants," Diego continues, with authority. "The bones were analyzed and found to be full of the carbon 13 isotope which is produced by corn. Corn is bad for the teeth and their teeth were full of cavities."

Still the guide says nothing.

"I liked the Virgins of the Sun theory," Irène says, laughing. "It's more romantic."

Irène met Diego at a polo match at the Lima Country Club, on a Sunday, Palm Sunday. Since Jeanne has the day off, Irène takes Liliane with her.

"You have to behave," she warns Liliane. "You cannot wander off. You have to hold my hand.

"Horses are dangerous," she adds.

Irène and Liliane watch the polo match standing on one side of the polo field—the side where the wives and friends of the polo players stand and the side where the grooms hold the

extra horses and equipment—only a few feet away from where
the game is being played. Horses gallop toward them and only
at what seems the last possible moment, their hooves clattering,
bridles jangling, do they stop short, wheel around, doing an intri-
cate quick dance of balance and of changing leads in midair on
their slender bandaged legs, then gallop off in another direction.

The sun is shining directly overhead. Both Irène and Liliane
wear hats—Irène a pretty straw hat, Liliane a babyish cotton one.
Once or twice, when the horses gallop toward them, Liliane's
face is sprayed with flecks from the sweat on the horses' necks
and this pleases her. She tries to lick the sweat off her cheek
with her tongue.

In between chukkers, the polo players ride over to where
Irène and Liliane are standing to change horses and, during the
break, before dismounting, one of the polo players smiles down
at Irène. During the next break, the same polo player reins in
his horse next to her and says something that Liliane does not
catch. His arms are brown and muscular, his teeth are very white.

"*Sí, claro. Diego*"—Yes, it's clear. Diego, Irène repeats, smiling.

Liliane watches him dismount and wipe his forehead with a
red kerchief, then take the bottle of water from his groom, drink
some, and spit out a mouthful. Liliane frowns at him—spitting
she knows is forbidden. He is wearing a green T-shirt with the
number 1 on the back and the T-shirt is stained with sweat.
Taking the reins of his new, fresh horse, a gray with red ribbons
tied in his braided mane, he mounts it with a single leap and
before he is properly settled in the saddle or his feet are in the
stirrups—the gray horse already turning, moving toward the
field in anticipation of the game—he waves his mallet at Irène.

*   *   *

"No one knows how the Inca builders carried the stones that weigh several tons up to Machu Picchu," the guide starts up again. "Or how they carved them without mortar. At the time, they had neither iron nor the wheel. Their only calculating system was based on knotted strings."

"Knotted strings," Irène repeats.

"The knotted string is called *quipu*," Diego, who, in addition to being a ranked polo player, is a banker, tells her. "A *quipu* is a storage device, not a calculator, and it consists of strings which are knotted to represent numbers, using a positional base 10 representation. For instance, if the Inca wanted to record the number 479, the nine touching knots were placed near the free end of the string, a space was left, then seven touching knots for the 10s, another space, and . . ."

Irène has never looked lovelier.

So far in Lima, Irène has managed to avoid her husband's relatives. She does not dislike her mother-in-law, but she dislikes her sister-in-law, Edith, and Edith's husband, Helmo. Peruvian by birth, Helmo nevertheless is German through and through. He and Edith are both staunchly, stubbornly patriotic at the same time that they are woefully out of touch. It is useless to discuss, argue, or exchange harsh words with them. Better to exchange no words at all.

Also, Irène never again wants to speak German—nor does she.

Irène's mother-in-law, Emilie, although assimilated and baptized a Lutheran, at heart, remains Jewish, but does not speak of it. Instead, she speaks of other things: her house in Lima with the interior tiled courtyard, her brilliant red geraniums, her Spanish lessons with Señorita Hernandez, her incontinent, old dachshund, Maxie, and her only grandchild, Liliane.

Emilie grew up in Hamburg and spent her summers on a large family estate in Schleswig-Holstein, called Dunkelsdorf. She is fond of telling stories describing the details either remembered or invented of her life there to Liliane: the all-white roses her mother grew in the garden, the mean little pony she was made to ride, a disturbingly gory painting attributed to Delacroix that hung in the somber dining room. Her descriptions also bring to life her sisters—Marguerite, the plump, kind one, and Friederike, the beautiful one—and the much indulged and admired handsome younger brother and, finally, Mademoiselle Armand, the temperamental, sharp-tongued French governess.

Mon dieu, les allemands! Les boches—My God, the Germans! The boches. . . .

"In addition to French, we learned English, Latin, and my brother's tutor taught us a bit of mathematics and philosophy. I'll never forget him. His name was Dietrich von Mendel; he had a degree from Heidelberg University. A very nice young man. I often wonder what became of him—whether he married and had children," Liliane's grandmother tells her, smiling.

Dietrich von Mendel is one of the five million German dead at the end of World War I.

Liliane is too young to notice the smile or the look in her grandmother's pale blue eyes (but nearsighted—Emilie's eyes are nearly hidden by the thick lenses of her glasses). And Liliane is not interested in the nice tutor from Heidelberg University;

instead she is interested in the pony her grandmother was made to ride.

"How was he mean?" she wants to know.

"He would reach around and try to bite me when I was getting ready to mount or he would buck to make me fall off."

"And did you?"

Liliane has a hard time picturing her grandmother young or on horseback.

On her visits to Emilie, which usually coincide with Jeanne's day off, Liliane also tries to play with Maxie. Inside the tiled courtyard, she throws a rubber ball for him but Maxie is too blind—cataracts have formed over his eyes—too lame, too indifferent to go after it.

"Fetch, Maxie, fetch," she shouts at him.

When she tries to pick him up in her arms, Maxie snaps at her.

"Careful," her grandmother says, "Maxie might bite you."

"Like your pony," Liliane says.

And, always, she begs her grandmother to tell her more stories.

On her days off, Jeanne leaves the house early to attend Mass at La Ermita, a red stone church a few miles from Miraflores in the Barranco district of Lima. To get there, she has to either take public transportation, the crowded, dirty bus or, if the chauffeur, Mañuel, is not occupied with driving Irène, beg a ride from him. The church, originally a fisherman's shrine, feels right to her. A miracle occurred there—something to do with fishermen lost at sea in the fog who see a light. The light comes from the cross on the church steeple and it guides the fishermen back to the safety of land. On her knees, on the cold stone floor, surrounded by burning candles, plastic flowers, and the ornately decorated plaster statues of saints, Jeanne, a scarf tied around her head, her eyes closed, prays for the safety of her family back in Brittany. Such a long time since she has seen or had any news that she has a hard time picturing them, especially the younger ones—no longer children, teenagers now. And do they do well in school? Jeanne wonders. Are they obedient to their parents, helping out at home: milking the cow, feeding the chickens? And what about her father? Is there enough gasoline to run the boat named after her mother—*Marie-Paul*—and for him to fish? And the others? Has Daniel married Suzanne as he hoped to? Perhaps, they have a child—Jeanne smiles at the thought.

But, when the war is over and she leaves Peru and returns to France, Jeanne will learn that Daniel was a soldier in one of the two French divisions that stayed behind on the beaches to protect the evacuation of Dunkirk and, afterward, had to surrender to the Germans. Taken to a forced-labor camp in Poland, Daniel never came back. No doubt he was one of the nearly 25,000 French prisoners of war to die of either malnutrition, overwork, or typhoid fever.

And is Catherine still teaching school? Jeanne continues to wonder. She can almost hear how the little village children call out excitedly when they see her—*Maîtresse! Maîtresse!*—Teacher! Teacher! And Annick? Has she dyed her hair red the way she has always threatened to? Again, Jeanne smiles. She also thinks about her mother, Marie-Paul, whom she loves very much. So many questions! And she prays hard to soon get answers. Getting up from her knees, she lights a candle for each of them.

Then, she goes to confession.

Mon père, j'ai péché—My father, I have sinned . . .

What sins can Jeanne possibly have to confess?

That she loses patience with Liliane when, to tease her, Liliane makes as if to pick something dirty from the ground.

That she pretends not to understand when the cook asks her to keep an eye on the rice boiling on the stove while she steps outside for a moment and the water boils over.

That she lets the chauffeur kiss her on the way back from La Ermita, but stops him when he tries to touch her breasts.

Non, non, Mañuel, she told him, pushing away his hand.

Leaning past Jeanne, Mañuel put his hand against the door handle, not letting her out of the car.

Un besos—a kiss, Mañuel demanded in return for letting her open the car door.

Poor Jeanne.

Her timid ways, her pale skin and glasses, her starched, spotless uniform, her not joining in with the jokes and complaints in the kitchen, which, in any event, she has difficulty understanding, her not eating the spicy food, the fried beans, the tough roasted corn, her keeping herself to herself.

When the polo game is over and Diego's team has won, Diego again rides over to where Irène is standing but, instead of dismounting, he reins in his horse and, pointing to Liliane with his whip, he says, "*La niña*"—the little girl.

Irène starts to shake her head, but already Liliane has let go of her hand and is reaching up to pat the horse's wet neck. Leaning down, Diego picks up Liliane and, in one effortless motion, he sets her down in front of him. Sensing a foreign presence, the horse shakes his head up and down, and Diego speaks sharply to him at the same time that he gives the horse a slight flick with his whip as they trot off onto the empty polo field.

Diego! Liliane hears Irène call out.

Diego has his arm firmly around Liliane's waist as she bounces uncomfortably on the horse's neck, but she doesn't mind.

Also, her cotton hat has come untied and falls to the ground and she is glad that Diego makes no move to retrieve it.

Diego! Irène calls again. Already, she sounds far away.

IV

In 1946, the war over, Rudy, Irène, and Liliane return to Paris and stay at the Hôtel Raphaël on the Avenue Kléber. Built in 1925, the hotel once boasted eighty-six luxurious bedrooms furnished with precious Oriental carpets, Louis XV antiques, and expensive velvet drapes, but by the time Rudy, Irène, and Liliane arrive, the carpets, the furniture, the drapes are definitely the worse for wear—as is the city, suffering still from the scarcities and deprivations caused by the German occupation.

During the war, senior German officers and staff members of the German Military Command had taken up residence in the best Paris hotels, the Crillon, the Meurice, the Lutetia, the George V, and the Raphaël—Hitler once dined with General Otto von Stülpnagel at the Hôtel Raphaël. One of the German officers staying at the Hôtel Raphaël was the Wehrmacht captain Ernst Jünger, an acclaimed but controversial writer, whose most popular and semi-autobiographical novel *Storm of Steel* was based on his World

War I experiences. Jünger was a regular presence at Parisian theater, cabarets, and expensive restaurants and he fraternized with such well-known French writers and artists as Sacha Guitry, Jean Cocteau, the French publisher Gaston Gallimard, Pablo Picasso, and the American heiress Florence Gould. He was also linked with the so-called Stauffenberg bomb plot, the assassination attempt on Hitler in 1944, by the anti-Nazi conservatives, a group of mostly old Prussian officers that included the German military commander in occupied France, General Carl-Heinrich von Stülpnagel (first cousin to Otto von Stülpnagel whom he succeeded), and the Supreme Field Commander West General Günther von Kluge. Many of the conspirators were said to be nervously awaiting the outcome of the assassination attempt at the Hôtel Raphaël and, afterward when it failed—four people were killed in the blast, including Hitler's stenographer, while Hitler only suffered scorched trousers and a perforated eardrum—Kluge committed suicide and Stülpnagel, after attempting to shoot himself and succeeding in only blinding himself, was hanged. Shortly after the Normandy landings, Jünger, who had never belonged to the Nazi Party, and was considered a "good German," managed to check out of the Hôtel Raphaël in time—paying his bill and leaving a bunch of flowers at the desk—and return to Berlin where, instead of being executed or punished, he was merely dismissed from the army. Banned from publishing for a few years, he was rehabilitated in the 1950s and went on to write and publish more than fifty books. He also lived to be 102.

Liliane goes to a small French school called Les Abeilles (The Bees) on Avenue Georges Mandel. Every morning, according to

the arrangement made by Rudy and Irène, and before he begins
his shift, Maurice, the one-armed hotel elevator man, walks her
there. On the way to school, his empty sleeve neatly folded and
tucked inside his uniform pocket, Maurice holds Liliane's hand
firmly in his and teaches her the words to songs:

> *Il etait un petit navire,*
> *Qui n'avait ja-ja jamais navigué,*
> *Ohé! Ohé! Ohé! Ohé! Matelot . . .*

> *There was once a little boat,*
> *That never had sailed,*
> *Ahoy! Ahoy! Ahoy! Ahoy! Sailor . . .*

and

> *Malbrouk s'en va-t-en guerre,*
> *Mironton, mironton, mirontaine,*
> *Ne sait quand reviendra,*
> *Ne sait quand reviendra*

> *Marlborough has gone to war,*
> *Mironton, mironton, mirontaine,*
> *Who know when he will come back,*
> *Who knows when he will come back*

In the first song, the youngest sailor picks the short straw
when the food on board the ship runs out and is chosen to be
eaten by the others; in the second song, the Duke of Marlborough has been killed in battle and will not be coming home to

his waiting wife. As Liliane sings along with Maurice, she would like to ask him how he lost his arm but she never does.

Mme Kantéronig, an elderly lady who no doubt has seen better days and is now reduced to earning her living as a governess, picks Liliane up from school. Together, they walk back to the Hôtel Raphaël. If the weather is fine and Mme Kantéronig has not forgotten to bring Liliane's roller skates, they stop off at the Trocadéro and Liliane can roller-skate on the broad terrace there; she can also roller-skate back to the hotel on the Avenue Kléber sidewalk—waiting at street crossings for Mme Kantéronig to catch up. In the evening, Liliane and Mme Kantéronig order from room service and eat dinner together.

The food at Les Abeilles is terrible—worse than terrible. A fish dish that one day, despite threats from the teacher in charge of the lunchroom, Liliane refuses to eat reappears for her at lunch the following day. The school has only a single WC for both the boys and the girls—a hole in the floor—and Liliane never goes. She holds it in all day. At the beginning of the school year, Liliane takes piano lessons but after three or four lessons, the teacher complains to Irène that Liliane is tone-deaf and that she is wasting her time and Irène her money and the lessons stop. In addition, Liliane, who is first put in *neuvième*, a class equivalent to the third grade, is soon demoted to *dixième*, equivalent to second grade, when it becomes clear that she does not know French grammar or how to spell. A black-and-white class photo shows a motley group of nine poorly dressed, spindly legged, undernourished-looking children. Only Liliane looks remotely robust.

* * *

Rudy and Irène have the adjoining bedroom to Liliane's in the Hôtel Raphaël. At night the door is kept shut, yet Liliane can hear them argue. She can also hear Rudy leave to spend the night elsewhere.

"*Chérie*, are you awake?" Irène says, opening the door that connects the two bedrooms.

Pretending to be asleep, Liliane does not answer.

Quietly, Irène comes over and kisses Liliane's cheek and Liliane has difficulty keeping her eyes shut and her breathing regular.

She can smell her mother's perfume. Always the same one—Joy, the most expensive perfume in the world; an ounce consists of ten thousand jasmine flowers and three hundred roses.

Where does Rudy go? Years later, he will stay at the Hôtel Royal Monceau, as elegant and expensive as the Hôtel Raphaël, and twice as large. During the Fontainebleau Conference, Ho Chi Minh spends nearly two months at the Royal Monceau while attempting to negotiate a peace agreement with the French; the negotiations for the Israeli Declaration of Independence that is eventually signed by David Ben-Gurion and Golda Meir take place in the hotel lounges; King Farouk of Egypt stays at the Royal Monceau as well—he takes up an entire floor of the hotel and once when Liliane accidentally gets off the elevator on King Farouk's floor, his Bedouin bodyguards, stationed in the hallway, indicate with menacing gestures that she must leave.

Although most of his work after the war is in Rome, Rudy, who has been made a French citizen, comes to Paris often on business. In addition to Astoria Films, his Italian film company, he has a French film company called Gladiator Productions, and the office, conveniently, is across the street from the Hôtel Royal Monceau, on Avenue Hoche.

Before the war, Rudy produces *La Maison du Maltais* (*Sirocco* in English) and *Le Dernier Tournant* (a French adaptation of *The Postman Always Rings Twice*) with Charles Smadja. Charles Smadja is the business associate who came to visit Rudy while he was interned at the camp in Marolles; Smadja is also the one who, during that troubled time, agreed to give Irène money—money that belonged to Rudy—so that she could leave the country on the condition that she sleep with him. Irène threatened to tell Rudy, but for some reason she never did.

After the war, Rudy works with Émile Natan, and together they produce the musical *Violettes Impériales* with the Basque singer Luis Mariano. Mariano seduces the Gypsy heroine Carmen Sevilla, in the title role, by repeatedly singing to her in his grating tenor voice:

L'amour est un bouquet de violette

Love is a bouquet of violets

They also produce *La Belle Otero* with María Félix playing the famous courtesan whose lovers—each of whom gave her a pearl necklace—included Prince Albert I of Monaco, King Edward VII of England, the king of Serbia, the king of Spain, and the Russian

Grand Dukes Peter and Nicholas. Men were said to have fought duels and/or committed suicide over Otero and a number of legends grew up around her, including the legend that the twin cupolas of the Hôtel Carlton in Cannes were modeled on her breasts. Otero amassed a huge fortune but gambled it all away and died in a state of poverty. "Women," she was supposed to have declared, "have one mission in life: to be beautiful. When they grow old, they must break all the mirrors."

Originally Romanian, Émile Natan is rugged and robust with unruly white hair. His wife, Monique, is the opposite: tiny, perfectly coiffed and dressed. Émile and Monique Natan live in an apartment filled with art—Liliane remembers a lovely Renoir painting of roses—on the Rond-Point des Champs-Élysées. She also remembers how Monique took her to Guerlain and bought her a bottle of Eau de Cologne Impériale—the perfume named for Napoleon III's wife, Empress Eugénie—and how, soon after, when Émile dies unexpectedly of a heart attack, Monique jumps to her death from the balcony of the apartment, holding her little dog, a white poodle, in her arms.

In Paris, Rudy's favorite restaurant is Chez Anna. It is located on Boulevard Delessert and owned and run by a diminutive and combative middle-aged woman named Anna. Anna wears a medical doctor's white smock and steel-rimmed glasses, her gray hair is pulled back in a tight chignon. She shouts at and insults her waiters, the cook, and, according to her mood—usually angry— or, on a whim, because she does not like the look of them or else, more charitably, because she thinks they can't afford her prices, turns down customers at the door claiming the restaurant is full when clearly it is nearly empty. Not so for Rudy. She loves Rudy. When Rudy arrives she makes a big fuss—hugging, kissing, and calling him "*Mon petit Rudy*" (although Rudy is twice as tall as Anna) or "*Mon Rudy chéri*." Anna orders for him. She brings a huge plate heaped with langoustines and a bowl filled with yellow homemade mayonnaise, a platter of plump, juicy white asparagus, fresh foie gras with thin slices of toasted bread, giant red radishes, and a dish of fresh butter; then, for the main course, bright pink slices of *gigot*, a creamy potato gratin, baby lima beans, and finally for dessert—for Liliane especially, if Rudy has brought her—a coupe filled with *fraises des bois*, topped with a big spoonful of crème fraîche; next to it, wrapped in gold paper, are two paper-thin cigarette cookies, which Liliane, still a child, pretends to smoke before eating them.

Every night at ten o'clock sharp, Anna's dog, a big brown poodle mix named Marcel, comes down the stairs from Anna's apartment above the restaurant and, with a single leap, jumps on top of the bar.

"I can set my watch by him," Rudy says.

"How does Marcel know the time?" Liliane asks.

Anna shrugs. "Marcel is very intelligent," and going over to the bar, she gives the dog a kiss, saying, *"Mon Marcel chéri."*

Rudy has a mistress in Paris. Her name, coincidentally, is Irina and she, too, is blonde and pretty—but not as pretty as Liliane's mother. She is Russian and married. Her husband is a professor and they have a son about whom Irina complains to Rudy. Alex is intelligent but lazy. He is sixteen years old and he still does not know what he is going to do. Irina is critical. She shows no interest in Liliane or in Liliane's life and Liliane does not like her. While they are having dinner together, Rudy speaks to Irina in Russian and Liliane is excluded. Afterward, they all three go back to the Hôtel Royal Monceau and, once inside, Rudy checks— Liliane hears him jiggle the doorknobs—to make sure that the double doors between their two rooms are locked. (Years later, Rudy leaves a letter instructing Liliane to give Irina five thousand dollars upon his death. But when Rudy dies, he no longer has five thousand dollars—or, for that matter, any money—and Liliane, feeling obliged to follow her father's last wishes while at the same time feeling deeply resentful, gives Irina the money out of her own pocket.)

In the fall of 1947, Liliane, who has just turned eight, and her mother leave France on a converted troopship operated by Moore-McCormack Lines. There is still a severe shortage of liners—only thirteen are in transatlantic operation (versus seventy-three before the war) and only two—the *Queen Elizabeth* and the *America*—of the thirteen are luxury liners. The rest are substandard and provide low-cost transportation. The fares range from $167 to $190 for the women and a flat fee of $127 for the men. The passengers sleep in open troop quarters that hold more than 100 passengers each. The sleeping berths are arranged in tiers of four; each berth has a mattress, clean linen, a blanket, a towel and a cake of soap. Arriving on board late, Irène and Liliane are unable to get berths on the same tier—the women already occupying the three others refuse to give up their space or to move. Liliane sleeps on an upper berth a few tiers away from Irène, who sleeps on the lowest berth on another tier. In the berth directly below Liliane, a woman has managed to smuggle in her two little dachshunds. The dachshunds whine restlessly during the night and keep Liliane awake. The overhead lights are kept on all day and all night and they, too, keep her awake. Irène, also, can't sleep and, most nights, she gets up at three or four in the morning to use the communal bathroom and to take a shower—at that hour, she has some privacy.

Most of the passengers on board are displaced persons— thus far, only 36,000 out of the near million Eastern European displaced persons have been allowed entry into the United States.

Fourteen-year-old Vera, who was sent to a forced-labor camp and whose parents were gassed, is one of them. She and Liliane play cards together. They play relentlessly all day, sitting cross-legged up on either Liliane's berth or on Vera's, also a top berth, without ever exchanging a single word—Liliane speaks only French and Spanish and Vera only Czech, except for when she shouts out, "*Va à la pêche!*"—Go fish!

"Can you stop playing for a bit and go up on deck and get some fresh air," Irène has to tell Liliane. "You'll get sick if you stay in this cabin all day," she adds. Also, Irène is not sure she likes for Liliane to spend so much time with Vera. Although not the girl's fault, Irène senses something feral and perverse about her. She imagines that Vera's experiences of deprivation and of, perhaps, beatings and rape in the labor camp will taint Liliane.

When Liliane goes up on deck, the air is humid; the ocean is relatively calm and a uniform gray. While she sits in a deck chair and reads her book, *Les Malheurs de Sophie* (*Sophie's Misfortunes*) by the Comtesse de Ségur, an account of the trifling misadventures of a little French girl who regularly disobeys her parents and suffers the consequences, a Hungarian boy, his arms flailing, jogs awkwardly around the deck past her. Like Vera, he is an orphan and a camp survivor. He looks to be about fifteen or sixteen and Liliane knows there is something wrong with him. Each time he runs by Liliane, he shouts something at her and Liliane, pretending to be absorbed in her book, does not look up. He frightens her. As Liliane shuts her book and gets ready to leave, the Hungarian boy comes around once again and, as if guessing her intention, he stops and stands directly in front of Liliane's chair. Then, before Liliane can move or say anything, the Hungarian boy drops his pants.

A heavyset Polish woman sleeps in the berth directly above Irène's and every night, around midnight, a man tiptoes into the room from the men's quarters and climbs into her berth. To do so, he first steps onto the edge of Irène's berth before he hoists himself up into the woman's berth, then the two have sex. Above Irène's head the berth shakes so violently she is afraid it will collapse on top of her. After a few minutes, the shaking stops then, almost immediately, the man leaves. Again, he steps down on the edge of Irène's berth. One night, a second man comes shortly after the first one has left and he, too, steps on the edge of Irène's berth before hoisting himself up into the Polish woman's berth.

The voyage takes eight long days.

"The ship was disgusting," Irène tells Gaby, her future husband, when finally they land in New York harbor. "A floating flophouse," she says. "*Un bordel*"—a brothel, she adds in French.

Irène is not anti-Semitic but she does not want to be reminded of some of her ancestors or of her roots. Her mother, born Louise Clara Ida Maria Sonnenburg was the daughter of Eduard Sonnenburg and Anna Marianne Caroline Westphal; Anna was the daughter of Carl Friedrich Otto Westphal, a neurologist and author of the popular yet troubling essay Die Konträre Sexualempfindung: Symptom eines neuropathololologischen ("The Opposing Sexual Instinct: A Symptom of Neuropathololology"), one of the first medical accounts of homosexuality as a psychiatric disorder, and Clara Rosamunde Dorothea Mendelssohn; Clara Mendelssohn was the daughter of Alexander Mendelssohn

who was the son of Joseph Mendelssohn, who, in turn, was the eldest son of Moses Mendelssohn.

Moses Mendelssohn was born in Dessau, Germany, in 1729. Despite many health problems, which included scoliosis, Moses learned the entire Bible by heart at the age of six. By the time he was fourteen—besides Yiddish, his first language—he spoke German, Latin, Greek, French, and English. Mostly self-taught, Moses never went to university nor did he ever hold an academic position. He supported himself by working in a silk factory. In 1762, he met and fell in love with Fromet Guggenheim, a young girl from Hamburg who was blonde and beautiful. However, when Fromet Guggenheim saw Moses Mendelssohn for the first time—she knew him by reputation only—and saw his stunted misshapen figure, she began to weep.

"Is it because of my hump?" Moses asked her.

"Yes," Fromet admitted tearfully.

"Let me tell you a story," he said.

"According to a Talmudic saying, a proclamation of the name of the person I will marry was made in heaven when I was born. Not only was my future wife named but it was also said that she would be hunchbacked. 'Oh, no,' I said to myself, 'she will be deformed, bitter and unhappy. Dear Lord,' I said again, 'give me the hump instead and make her fair and beautiful.'"

Fromet was so moved by Moses's story that she dried her tears and they married. She and Moses lived together happily and had ten children, six of whom survived to adulthood.

Known both as the German Socrates and the Jewish Luther, Moses Mendelssohn is considered to be the founding father of Jewish philosophy and Jewish Enlightenment. He was also an accomplished literary critic and translator—he translated the first five books of the Hebrew Bible known as the *Pentateuch* and the *Psalms* into High German. During his lifetime, Moses Mendelssohn was best known for his accounts of the experience of the sublime and for his arguments on the soul's immortality and God's existence. Today Moses Mendelssohn is probably best known for his tireless attempts to reform Jewish ideals by stressing religious tolerance, the importance of secular knowledge, and material happiness.

Mendelssohn's most important works are *Phädon or On the Immortality of Souls; Bi'ur (Elucidation); Jerusalem;* and *Morning Hours, or Lectures on the Existence of God*. He expressed some of his beliefs thus:

A God is thinkable, therefore a God is also actually present.

State and church have a duty to promote, by means of public measures, human felicity in this life and in the future life.

With regard to man, we believe that he was created in God's image, yet that he is a human being—that is, that he is liable to sin. We know nothing of original sin. Adam and Eve sinned because they were human beings and died because they sinned. And so it goes with all their descendants. They sin and die.

Formerly, every imaginable effort was made and various measures were taken to turn us not into useful citizens, but into Christians. And since we were so stiff-necked and stubborn as to not allow ourselves to be converted, this was reason enough to regard us as a useless burden to the world and to attribute to such depraved monsters all the horrors that could only subject them to the hatred and contempt of all people. Now the zeal for conversion has subsided, and we are completely neglected. People continue to distance us from all the arts and sciences as well as the other useful professions and occupations of mankind. They bar us from every path to useful improvement and make our lack of culture the reason for oppressing us further. They tie our hands and reproach us for not using them.

Always frail, Moses Mendelssohn died in 1786; of his six children, only his daughter Recha and son Joseph continued to practice Judaism; Joseph's son, Alexander, was the last Mendelssohn descendant to keep the Jewish faith.

While Liliane is growing up, no one mentions Judaism. No one talks about being Jewish. Irène never does, nor does Rudy. By then, they are both Lutherans, but neither one is religious. (Once married to Gaby, Irène occasionally, in the summer, goes to an Episcopal church on an island in Maine. As for Rudy, except to have some peace and quiet in Marolles or to sightsee in Rome, he never steps foot inside either a church or a synagogue.) Is it a cover-up or a form of anti-Semitism? More likely—and more generously—Liliane thinks her parents were blocking out the horror of the Holocaust by not discussing their past. Also, and she has read this explanation: "The survivors are focused on building a new life in a new country with all the difficulties that come with that, where you don't have the language and the customs. That process is 'future oriented,' unlike mourning."

Irène's side of the family converted several generations ago when Clara, Alexander Mendelssohn's daughter, married Carl West-phal, while it is not clear when the conversion takes place on Rudy's side. When Emilie marries? And is Felix, her husband, already a Christian? In imperial Germany, Jews rarely became professors unless they were baptized. Again, Emilie never speaks of it. The only evidence Liliane has is a long white lace christening dress that her father, Rudy, wore in 1908 to receive the sacrament of baptism at a church in Bonn. Thirty-or-so years later, in Paris, Liliane, too, wears the same white lace dress to be christened and, according to Lutheran practice, to be cleansed from sin, snatched from the power of Satan and given everlasting life.

On Irène's father side, the family genealogy is more complex and less direct, but it is the one that Irène likes to lay claim to as it is glamorous and goes all the way back to Mary, Queen of Scots.

Waldemar was the son of Baroness Auguste Wilhelmine von Egloffstein, whose husband was the son of Baroness Marie Karoline von Egloffstein, whose husband, in turn, was the Baron Friedrich August von Egloffstein. He was the son of Lady Elisabeth MacCarthy, who was the daughter of Donough MacCarthy, 3rd Earl of Clancarty, whose mother was Elisabeth Spencer and whose father was Robert, Earl of Sunderland. Robert had a son, Charles Spencer, 3rd Earl of Sunderland, who married Lady Anne Churchill. Their grandson, George Spencer, 5th Duke of Marlborough, took on the additional name of Churchill in 1817. It is here that the branches of the Spencer family tree become tangled with those of the Churchill family and suffice it to say that a century earlier Arabella Churchill was the mistress of James II, Stuart king of England. She had four children by him; James II, in a penultimate turn, was the grandson of James I, king of England, and he, of course, was Mary Stuart's son.

Beheaded on February 8, 1587, on an unusually sunny day, which was thought to be a sign of accord from the heavens, Mary, Queen of Scots was forty-four years old when she died. With the first blow of the axe, the executioner, a Mr. Bull, missed Mary's neck and instead sliced open the top of her head. Her lips were seen to move. When, finally, the bloody deed was done and the executioner held up Mary's head for the crowd to see, her long auburn hair fell off in his hand. Mary had been wearing a wig; her own hair was short and gray. Also, curiously, her little dog, a Skye terrier, who, unperceived, had been hiding underneath Mary's skirts during the entire execution, suddenly emerged from the folds of her petticoats and lay down next to his mistress's corpse.

*   *   *

Josephine Baker is another important woman in Rudy's life
because, in 1941, she saved it. After being discharged from the
Foreign Legion and while he is stuck at the Hôtel de Noailles
in Marseille, without a passport or papers and waiting to leave
France to rejoin Irène and Liliane in Peru, Rudy happens to run
into Daniel Marouani, a well-known agent for review and music
hall artists who has retired in Nice. Rudy has had previous deal-
ings with Marouani, and Marouani explains that he is waiting for
Josephine Baker, his most important client, who is due to arrive by
train with her friend, Jacques Abtey, a captain in the French Army.

"Ah, Josephine Baker," Rudy tells Marouani with a smile.
"I knew her in Paris."

"Well, you will have a chance to see her again in a few
minutes if the train is on time," Marouani replies.

As it turns out, Josephine and Jacques are staying in the
same hotel as Rudy and, that evening, they have a drink together
in the bar. From then on, they have drinks and dinner together
every night. Soon they are inseparable and when Josephine has to
go to Nice for a week to perform *La Créole,* she insists that Rudy
come with her and Jacques. She promises Rudy he will be safe
with them. Finally, when the time comes for Josephine and Jacques
to leave France for North Africa, Josephine insists that she cannot
leave without her friend Rudy and she promises him that she will
get him a passport and visas. Josephine also insists that she cannot
leave France without her three pet monkeys—this proves easier
to arrange than getting Rudy a passport—and someone is sent
to Les Milandes, Josephine's house in the Dordogne, to fetch the
monkeys. Rudy is sorry to see Josephine and Jacques leave; he is

also apprehensive. Any day, he thinks, the authorities are going to come for him and deport him back to Germany. Fortunately, he is wrong. In his journal Rudy writes:

> I returned one night to the hotel and the concierge said to me: There is a man waiting for you. Normally, in my circumstances, I was not keen about visits from a stranger, but I told myself: If they have come to get you, usually they come in the morning and usually they don't come alone. I therefore went up to the man and said: You are looking for me? Without saying a word, the man put his hand in his pocket and took out a passport. Josephine and Jacques had kept their word; they had managed to open the door for me to life and liberty.

Rudy then joins Josephine, Jacques, and the three pet monkeys in Marrakesh, where Josephine had rented an Arab-style house in the medina. Although the house is charming, Rudy complains about the lack of water and the mosquitoes. He also complains about the pet monkeys. The monkeys crap inside the house and, one day, Rudy has had enough—barefoot, he nearly stepped in the mess—and he is determined to teach the monkeys a lesson. He waits until they again crap in the house, then grabbing each monkey by the neck, he spanks him hard on the bottom and throws him out the window—the Arab-style house is one-story. From then on, the monkeys continue to crap inside the house but when they are done, they spank their own bottoms and jump out the window.

It was also in Marrakesh that Rudy learns that Josephine and Jacques are working for the Deuxième Bureau, the French intelligence service. Together they had traveled through Spain and Portugal, ostensibly for Josephine's performances, with Jacques posing as her secretary, while secretly gathering information about the movement of the German military that they wrote down in invisible ink on Josephine's music scores.

Josephine Baker claimed that she had learned how to dance by watching animals in the zoo—especially the kangaroos. Uninhibited, she danced bare-breasted wearing only a bunch of feathers and shaking her *dérrière* at a dizzying speed, declaring, "The rear end exists. I see no reason to be ashamed of it. It's true there are rear ends so stupid, so pretentious, so insignificant that they're good only for sitting on." She clowned her way to success by making faces and crossing her eyes. Moving to Paris in 1925, Josephine joined the Folies Bergère, where she first starred as a native girl, climbing out of a jungle tree wearing a skirt made out of fake bananas. She had many lovers, including the entertainer Jacques Pills, Édith Piaf's future husband, and the writer Georges Simenon. According to an interview, Baker's beauty advice was to sweat and dance a lot.

Years later, in Paris, Rudy takes Liliane to one of Josephine's farewell performances, of which there are many. By then, Josephine Baker is in her fifties and has her "Rainbow Tribe" of children to support—twelve in all. She is overweight, nearsighted, and running out of money. But the show is a celebration, an extravaganza. Once onstage, a transformation takes place: swathed in furs, plumes, and glitter, Josephine sheds pounds, wrinkles, her glasses, and turns into a dazzling and alluring woman. The process has to do with showmanship, some inner magic, and her own special star quality. During the performance, Josephine dances, talks, improvises, and, finally, she sings:

> *I have two loves,*
> *My country and Paris.*
> *By them forever*
> *My heart is ravished.*

Applauding wildly, the audience adores her.

After the performance, Liliane and her father go backstage and Liliane sees how happy Josephine is to see Rudy.

"Rudy!" she cries, rushing up to embrace him.

"Josephine!" Rudy says, wiping tears from his eyes.

Liliane has never seen her father cry.

V

Pictures of horses cover the walls of Liliane's bedroom in the apartment in New York City. A Currier and Ives print titled *A Champion Horse Race* hangs across from her bed and depicts two horses, a bay and a black, racing neck and neck, as the drivers whip them on. Lying in bed, Liliane stares up at the print and tries to decide which of the two horses will win—she decides on the black. The other horse pictures in her room are sentimental drawings by the illustrator C. W. Anderson: *A Star Is Born* shows a newborn foal lying next to its mother while the mare grazes unconcernedly, *Good Advice* shows a mare nuzzling her foal, *Mares Running Their Colts* shows two foals gamboling in the foreground while the two mares are trotting behind, and, in *Siesta*, a foal is lying alone in the grass, apparently asleep, but, to Liliane, the foal looks dead.

Liliane, like many middle-class teenage white girls in North America, is horse crazy.

"Why can't you take up tennis, like your mother?" Gaby, her stepfather, asks, not expecting a reply. He is not familiar with Anna Freud's theories, popular at the time, that attempt to explain why the rhythmic movement of the horse reveals a young girl's autoerotic desires or why, again, grooming and saddling the horse reveal the girl's identification with her mother or why, yet again, her identification with the horse reveals her penis envy or why, still yet again, her phallic sublimations reveal her wish to control and master the horse.

In an attempt to answer his question, Liliane, after hesitating, says something vague about freedom—the freedom she experiences as she gallops across fields, the exhilaration she feels as she jumps fences.

"Horseback riding," she also says, "makes me feel strong."

But, by then, her stepfather is no longer listening to her; he is mixing himself another bourbon and water.

Once a week, Liliane goes to Boots and Saddles, a riding school housed in a defunct brewery—the indoor ring still smells of beer—on the Upper East Side of Manhattan. Her horse is a powerful, seventeen-hand bay named Mishka—the Russian diminutive for bear. The riding teacher is the handsome son of a Crimean prince, rumored to be a descendant of Genghis Khan. Tall, dark-haired, with high cheekbones and slightly slanted eyes—no doubt an adaptive advantage against the Siberian sleet and snow that harks back to his Mongol heritage—and impeccably dressed in his khaki shirt and tie, jodhpurs, and polished black riding boots, the handsome son is, in fact, called Chingis, a homonym for Genghis.

Stern and imperious, Chingis stands in the center of the ring; whip in hand, he barks out commands to the riders.

"Tighten up your reins," he shouts. "This is not a picnic ride."

Raising his whip in the air and advancing toward Liliane, he says, "Keep him moving, keep him moving. What are your heels for?"

Liliane is both attracted to and afraid of Chingis and while she rides—heels and hands down, seat firm, back straight, cantering round and round the ring, making figure eights, changing leads—she conflates him with his cruel and violent ancestor and fantasizes about being his favorite wife.

Wearing a flowing white tunic and a bright silk turban, she effortlessly keeps up with Genghis as they gallop across the barren Gobi Desert and as he vanquishes one disparate tribe after the other: the Merkits, the Naimans, the Mongols, the Keraits, the Tatars, and the Uighurs. She does not tire or complain. She does not complain when they must subsist only on yak's milk, or when, on occasion, to fortify himself, Genghis opens up a horse's vein and drinks the—

"How many times do I have to tell you not to shift your weight?" Chingis says, startling her. He sounds angry. "Leg pressure is enough."

About Chingis's private life, she knows nothing except for a fact he volunteers one day as he leaves class: "I have to go home and feed my chickens."

"Chickens? What kind of chickens?" Liliane asks.

"Sumatra. A rare breed from the Far East. But not friendly. The rooster, especially. The rooster attacks if anyone approaches the coop."

"Do the chickens lay eggs?" Liliane also asks.

Chingis shakes his head and laughs. "Rarely," he answers. And rarely, too, has Liliane seen him laugh.

A few weeks later, after class, he hands Liliane an egg. "Here, I brought you this," he tells her.

The egg is small and nasty and has specks of blood in it. Still, Liliane feels compelled to boil and eat it. She would like to believe that the gift of the egg is significant—don't the Russians, at Easter, exchange elaborately decorated eggs as tokens of love and friendship?

Wearing gold coins in her hair, she gallops alongside Genghis across the Kyzyl Kum Desert, where, at midday, the temperature soars to 125 degrees Fahrenheit. Accompanied by his soldiers and by wagons filled with their plunder—silk, rugs, wine, spices, perfume, silver—they are returning victorious from razing the cities of Bukhara, Samarkand, and Gurganj, after massacring all the inhabitants—

"Hey," Chingis shouts, cracking his whip at Mishka. "Stop daydreaming and keep your horse in line with the others."

The whip lands across Mishka's hindquarters. Mishka bucks, then bolts forward and Liliane falls off. She lands hard on her back. Gasping, she tries to get up and catch her breath. Putting his arms around her shoulders, Chingis helps Liliane to her feet; for a moment, he holds her.

For a long time afterward, Liliane relives this moment and embellishes on it.

Poor, proud, handsome Chingis, one of roughly sixteen million men carrying nearly identical Y chromosomes (the result of the rape and slaughter with which Genghis Khan founded the

Mongol Empire); he has no immediate family, he never marries and dies alone in a freak riding accident—electrocuted by a felled wire—thus confirming the old Russian saying (Said by whom? Said by her father's friend Tolia?) that a bachelor's life is a good life but he has a dog's death as no one is there to grieve for him, while a married man leads a dog's life but his death is pleasant as he is surrounded by his loved ones.

Genghis Khan's death was also caused by a riding accident —in his case, a fall from his horse. His body was brought back in a cart to his birthplace near Ulan Bator in Mongolia. By then, 1227, his empire extended across Asia, from the Pacific Ocean to the Caspian Sea. According to Genghis's wishes, his death was to be kept secret. Thus, anyone unlucky enough to meet the funeral procession along the way was killed—innocent little children, pregnant women, old people, it made no difference who they were. Once Genghis was buried, a herd of horses galloped back and forth over the grave site to hide any trace of it. A forest of trees was planted and soldiers were stationed there until the trees had grown sufficiently tall to completely conceal the spot. These strategies were so successful that, to this day, no one knows where Genghis Khan is buried.

Liliane is sixteen when she sees her first dead person. Her grandmother, Louise. Notwithstanding the winters she spent in Nice basking in the Mediterranean sunshine, Louise never fully recovered from the deprivations she endured in Innsbruck during the war, nor from her depression. Her letters to her daughter, Irène, were loving and always about the weather:

My darling Rehlein, It has rained all day for the past week . . .

My dearest Rehlein, The sun is struggling to come out but it is still cold and windy . . .

Rehlein, my darling, The weather has been unusually cold this spring and I can't seem to get warm . . .

Fittingly, on an unseasonally chilly and rainy day in July, Louise dies in a nursing home in Königstein, Germany. Alerted too late, Irène flies from New York and Liliane flies from Rome to join her mother. Louise is lying on a cot in a basement room of the nursing home. She is dressed in a skirt and print silk blouse, only her swollen feet are bare and Liliane cannot help but notice her toenails, which are painted pink. The polish is old and chipped and this, a sign of neglect, more than her grandmother's death, makes her sad. Louise's eyes are shut and her nostrils are stuffed with cotton; rouge has been applied to her cheeks. Taking one of her mother's hands—the fingernails, too, are painted with the same chipped pink polish—Irène puts the hand to her lips and covers it with noisy kisses, then she starts to cry. Embarrassed, Liliane looks away.

Liliane likes her other grandmother, Emilie, better.

After the war and after Maxie, the incontinent dachshund, is long dead, Emilie moves from the house with the interior tiled courtyard filled with brilliant red geraniums in Lima, to a one-bedroom apartment on Stewart Avenue, across from the noisy Alpha Delta Phi fraternity house, in Ithaca, New York. The reason Emilie moves to Ithaca is that her eldest son, Rudy's brother and Liliane's uncle, is a professor at Cornell.

Uncle Fritz to Liliane, but to scholars he is better known as a philologist, a classicist, and as "one of the last giants of

the German tradition of classical humanism." At Humboldt
University in Berlin—home to twenty-nine Nobel Prize win-
ners, including Albert Einstein and Max Planck, as well as to
some of Germany's greatest minds, such as G. W. F. Hegel,
Arthur Schopenhauer, Walter Benjamin, Karl Marx, Friedrich
Engels, the poet Heinrich Heine, and, last but not least, Otto
von Bismarck—Fritz studied with Werner Jaeger and Ulrich von
Wilamowitz-Moellendorff, both famous classical philologists.
The latter assembled a group of eminent young scholars—Fritz
among them—known as the Graeca, at his home to read and
edit Greek texts.

In 1932, Fritz marries one his students, Lieselotte Salzer,
a Lutheran from the city of Karlsruhe. A year later, they leave
Germany for England, then, in 1937, they manage to get to the
United States. Fritz teaches at Olivet College in Michigan before
moving to Cornell, where he will remain for the next twenty-two
years, heading the Classics Department, publishing more than

a hundred books, monographs, scholarly articles, and reviews on Aristotle, Plato, Cicero, Homer, Aeschylus, Hesiod, and other Greek and Roman writers, and, of course, teaching. One of his courses, Foundations of Western Thought, is especially popular and, according to the college catalogue, explores the history of philosophical, scientific, and religious ideas from early Greece through the Hellenistic and Roman periods.

Fritz smokes a pipe and, like his brother, Rudy, suffers from gout. Liliane has never heard him raise his voice or say an unkind word. He and Lieselotte live in a modest but comfortable brown stucco house on Wait Avenue, near enough to the Cornell campus so that Fritz can walk to work. A good cook and a good academic wife, Lieselotte entertains faculty members and is a respected civic-minded member of the community. Several days a week, she volunteers at the Tompkins County animal shelter. She and Fritz own a much admired Persian cat, called Pamphile—also admired by Vladimir Nabokov, who taught at Cornell for several years and was a neighbor—and named after the woman said to have invented silk weaving on the Greek island of Kos. Few incidents upset Fritz and Lieselotte's routine—a problem does arise with the neighbors over the property line—and, on the whole, life in Ithaca is peaceful, intellectually rewarding, and almost far enough removed from the events in Europe; and they have no children.

Fritz has his work, his students, and his colleagues, two of whom are his close friends: Jim Hutton and Harry Caplan. Tall, quiet, Jim Hutton, a lifelong bachelor, lives with his mother. His best-known works are his two studies on the influence of the Greek Anthology, *The Greek Anthology in Italy* and *The Greek Anthology in France and in the Latin Writers of the Netherlands to the Year 1800*; his numerous articles and reviews deal with subjects that range from classical antiquity to the twentieth century as, for example, his elegant and erudite sixty-three-page "Some English Poems in Praise of Music," a study of sixteenth- and seventeenth-century English poems on music that traces the historical tradition of the spheres. Harry Caplan is short, exuberant, and social. His field of study is ancient, medieval, and Renaissance rhetoric, the history of preaching and the intellectual history of the Middle Ages and the Renaissance. His greatest contribution to scholarship is his English translation of Cicero's *Rhetorica ad Herennium* for the Loeb Classical Library Series. Like Jim Hutton, Harry Caplan is a bachelor, only he lives alone. He tells jokes and makes a fuss over Liliane when she comes to Ithaca to visit; Jim Hutton is more reticent.

"Who do you like best?" Liliane asks her uncle. "Professor Hutton or Professor Caplan?"

Fritz laughs and shakes his head. "I like them both."

Determined to make him choose, Liliane persists, "You must like one better than the other."

"I like each in a different way," Fritz says.

"You have to have a best friend." Liliane refuses to give up.

In answer, Fritz laughs again.

Professor Hutton, she decides.

Liliane knows nothing about Lieselotte's family, nor did Lieselotte ever speak of them—mother, father, sisters, brothers—whoever stayed behind in Karlsruhe; a city with a grand palace and magnificent gardens built in the shape of a fan; a city that was heavily bombed during World War II and whose Jewish population was exterminated. And what could have Lieselotte said—and to whom?—when she received a telegram with the news that her younger brother, Ernst, a gunner in the German Luftwaffe, was killed on July 16, 1942? And how did she mourn him? Behind a closed bedroom door on a hot, airless summer afternoon thousands of miles away in Ithaca, New York? The only sound came from the sprinkler outside on the lawn as, every few seconds, water splashed against the leaves of the peony bushes Lieselotte planted on the sunny side of the house.

Sterbeurkunde G 2

(Standesamt IV München - - - - - - Nr. 2364/1942)

Der Gefreite der Technischen Kompanie Ing.d.E.-Stelle der Luftwaffe Ernst Friedrich Karl S a l z e r , Diplomingenieur, evangelisch - - - - -

wohnhaft in München - - - - - - - - - - - - -

ist am 16. Juli 1942 - - - gegen 08 Uhr- - - - Minuten in München Eid-Fjord bei Bergen/Norwegen - - - - - -

- verstorben.

D er Verstorbene war geboren am 15. Juli 1912 - - - - - - in Karlsruhe. - - - - - - - - - - - - - - - - - -

- -

D er Verstorbene war – nicht – verheiratet . - - - - - - - -

- - - - - - - - - - - - - - - - - - - -

München, den 18. April 1957.

Der Standesbeamte
In Vertretung

Scheithaler Hö

Gebühr - -50 DM
durch Postnachnahme erhoben.

Ernst, as his name implies, was an earnest and studious young boy but what Lieselotte remembers best about him is his voice. A member of the boys' choir, Ernst sang every Sunday in Karlsruhe's ancient Lutheran church and Lieselotte could still hear those transcending, treble voices:

Salvator mundi, salva nos,
Qui per crucem et sanguinem redemisti nos,
auxiliare nobis, te deprecamur, Deus noster.

Savior of the world, save us,
Who through thy cross and blood didst redeem us:
Help us, we beseech thee, our God.

Years later, when Harry Caplan dies, a letter he has kept for sixty-one years, dated March 27, 1919, is found in his desk drawer. The letter offers career advice and was written by his college teacher while he was a student at Cornell and goes in part like this: *The opportunities for college positions, never too many, are at present few and likely to be fewer. . . . There is moreover, a very real prejudice against the Jew. . . . I feel it wrong to encourage anyone to devote himself to the higher walks of learning to whom the path is barred by an undeniable racial prejudice.*

Fritz's best friend, Liliane decides, changing her mind, was Professor Caplan.

Once Liliane is ten years old she travels alone to visit her grandmother in Ithaca during her school holidays. From Pennsylvania Station, she takes the Lehigh Valley Railroad overnight Black Diamond Express, so named because the original train service was conceived to haul anthracite and other coal from Athens, Pennsylvania, to North Fair Haven, New York, on Lake Ontario. Liliane's Pullman sleeping car consists of two rows of double-decker berths that are enclosed for privacy by thick dark green curtains. She always chooses an upper berth and Wyngate, always the same porter, brings out a little ladder he affixes to a rung at the bottom of the berth for Liliane to climb up. Once inside, Liliane half undresses and puts her toiletries and her book, a Nancy Drew mystery, in the little string basket that hangs from the wall; the reading light is right over her head and, on the train, she looks forward to reading for as long as she likes. As soon as the train leaves Pennsylvania Station, she carefully unwraps the pack of Life Savers her mother has given her for the journey and sucks on one—lemon, her favorite—at the same time that she listens for Wyngate to walk down the corridor of the sleeping car. When, at last, she hears him, Liliane sticks her arm through the curtains and holds out the pack of Life Savers for him to take one and he does.

Always, too, in the morning, Wyngate accompanies Liliane to the dining car and finds her a seat at a table. On one of her trips a heavyset man wearing thick black-rimmed glasses and reading a magazine sits across from her. The magazine has a picture of two butterflies on the cover and is French: *Annales de la Société Entomologique de France*. Putting down the magazine, the man smiles at Liliane.

"I recommend the scrambled eggs," he tells her.

After Liliane has ordered breakfast, he asks her how old she is, what grade she is in, and what she studies in school.

He speaks with an accent that Liliane cannot place.

Then he asks, "What do you want to be when you grow up?"

"A writer," Liliane answers.

"How interesting." Again the man smiles at Liliane. "I'm a writer. I tell you what," the man continues, "I am going to write down my name and address on a piece of paper and when you are a little older and you have written something, you can send it to me."

"I will, I promise," Liliane says, pleased, as she takes the piece of paper the man hands her.

When Liliane gets off the train in Ithaca, her grandmother is waiting for her at the station.

"Did you have a good trip?" Emilie asks.

"Did you sleep on the train?"

"Have you had breakfast?"

When Liliane shows her grandmother the piece of paper with the name and address of the man she met on the train, her grandmother takes the piece of paper from Liliane and, without looking at it, rips it in half and throws it into a trash can.

* * *

In the Stewart Avenue apartment, Liliane sleeps on a fold-up bed in the same room as her grandmother. Emilie has strung two sheets on a line to divide the room and provide some privacy. The sheets are only partly effective. Through a crack, Liliane, who is pretending to already be asleep, can watch her grandmother undress. She watches as Emilie takes off her petticoat, her corset, her girdle—old-fashioned, faded pink garments that Liliane is not familiar with—and as, at the last moment, perhaps sensing that Liliane is watching her, Emilie slips her nightgown over her head without exposing any more bare flesh.

Liliane has no idea how old Emilie is. As far as Liliane is concerned, she could be any age—sixty, seventy. In fact, Emilie is nearly eighty. A plain-looking, opinionated, energetic woman, she grows an assortment of plants on her windowsills—she saves coffee grounds and eggshells to fertilize them—paints brilliant flowers in oils on shirt cardboards to save money, listens to a classical music station on the radio each afternoon, and insists, no matter what the weather, on walking several miles a day.

"It's too cold, I'm tired, it's boring," Liliane tells her grandmother. She does not want to walk.

"I'll tell you a story. You'll see the time will go by quickly," Emilie says, putting on her coat, her hat and gloves, and taking her cane, and Liliane has no choice but to follow her. As they start to cross the Stewart Avenue Bridge before heading up the steep hill toward Cayuga Heights, Liliane takes her grandmother's arm and Emilie, as promised, begins to tell a story.

Emilie's stories are all true.

"In 1848, my father, your great-grandfather, Rudolf Brach, left the village of Alzey where he was born and where he had always lived—"

"Alzey?" Liliane asks. "Where is that?"

"A small town in Germany, between the cities of Worms and Mainz, in the Rhine wine-growing district. But let me continue.

"—where he lived with his widowed mother and his younger sister—"

"What were their names?"

"Stop interrupting—my grandmother's name was Rachel and her daughter's name was Friederike."

"And what happened to them?"

"Friederike married a professor in Heidelberg. She died young."

"Did she have any children?"

"Yes, she had two sons, Friedrich and Rudolph."

"What happened to them?"

Emilie is shaking her head. "So many questions. They were raised by their stepmother. Friedrich was a respected rabbi in Heidelberg. His daughter went to live in Scotland, in Glasgow; his son was killed in World War I."

"What about Rudolph?"

Emilie stops for a moment on the bridge and leans heavily on her cane. Not looking at Liliane, she says, "Rudolph also lived in Heidelberg, he was a lawyer. He and his wife died in Auschwitz. His daughter and her husband died in Bergen-Belsen."

The deck truss bridge suddenly feels insubstantial and, below, the falling water in the gorge sounds unusually loud and rushed. Peering down, Liliane briefly contemplates what it might be like to jump.

Emilie resumes walking and Liliane does not say anything.

"As I was saying," Emilie says after a few minutes.

"When Rudolf Brach left his home to go to America, he traveled by Rhine paddle steamer first to Rotterdam, then on to Le Havre, where he boarded an American ship called the *Mayflower*—"

"The *Mayflower*?" Liliane frowns.

"A different *Mayflower*," Emilie answers, smiling.

"How old was Rudolf Brach?"

"He was young. Nineteen."

"The steward on board the ship was black. Except for the colored men Rudolf had seen at country fairs, who ate live chickens, feathers and all, the steward was the first black man Rudolf had ever seen up close—"

"Is this true? Or are you making this up?" Liliane asks.

"It's quite true," Emilie says. "I promise."

"The steward was lazy and did not make up Rudolf's bed or clean his cabin the way he was supposed to. The captain, too, got impatient and angry at the steward. He once threw a chair at him. The sailors were a motley and surly lot. In addition to the cargo, there were over two hundred people in steerage, mostly Germans—men, women, and young children. The voyage to New Orleans took forty days and during a lot of the time, Rudolf was seasick. To make matters worse, the food on board was terrible. The passengers had to live on salt pork, black potatoes, almonds, and raisins."

Liliane makes a face.

"Once he arrived in New Orleans, Rudolf went ashore and, as luck would have it, the first person he ran into turned out to be his uncle, Joseph Hernsheim, who, with his wife and children, had settled there and whom Rudolf was going to meet. Joseph Hernsheim owned a ready-made clothing business—mostly cheap cotton goods. This uncle gave Rudolf fifty dollars, more money than Rudolf had ever held in his hand, and made him a partner. Then Rudolf set off for Mexico to sell his wares."

"Did Rudolf speak Spanish?" Liliane asks.

She has a horror of speaking another language in America: of drawing attention to herself and of being labeled a foreigner. She wants to fit in or else disappear—vanish into thin air.

If her mother speaks to her in French in public, Liliane refuses to answer. When they first arrive in New York City, Irène and Liliane mistakenly climb on the Madison Avenue bus by the rear door—the way they board the bus in Paris. Catching sight of them, the bus driver stops the bus, gets out of his seat, walks back to where Irène and Liliane are standing, and, in front of the other passengers, he calls them cheaters, he calls them dishonest; then, he makes them get off the bus.

"Damn stupid foreigners," the bus driver yells after them.

In school, her first year, until she can manage a perfect English sentence, Liliane does not once open her mouth to speak. She is in third grade and the class is studying the Egyptians—that much Liliane can tell because student drawings of pyramids, Egyptian gods and goddesses, and hieroglyphs are pasted on the walls of the classroom. The teacher, too, ignores her.

* * *

Liliane and Irène share a fourth-floor walk-up apartment in midtown with a Miss Beecroft. Miss Beecroft is a mystery. It is never clear what role Miss Beecroft plays in their lives or what her relationship to Irène is. Or how they met. Miss Beecroft is English and works in an office during the day and comes home in the evening. She is in her fifties, overweight, and a spinster. She and Liliane have supper together as Irène is often out. Liliane has no strong feelings of either like or dislike for Miss Beecroft. All she knows is that after Irène and Gaby get married, they never see Miss Beecroft again.

During that first year in New York, Irène works modeling coats for a fur company located downtown in the garment district. Since she does not have proper working papers or a green card, Irène is fortunate to have a job. Her employers, Lena and Niko, husband and wife, are of Russian descent and pride themselves on running a family business that has been in existence since 1910. Lena, jealous, is quick to chastise Irène if, after taking Liliane to school, she is late; Niko, on the other hand, adjusting a lapel as a pretext, fondles Irène's breast. He also pays Irène in cash and lets her buy a mink coat at a discount.

Irène wears the mink coat when she goes to St. John's, Newfoundland. She tells her employers that her visa for the United States has expired and she has to leave the country for a few days. The real reason she leaves is to get an abortion. She takes Liliane with her and they stay in a hotel. The only thing Irène tells Liliane is that she has to see a doctor and the doctor's two teenage boys will look after her while Irène is gone. Liliane does not question what she is told. On the day of the abortion, the two teenage boys come to the hotel and take Liliane skating. The two boys look nearly identical; they both wear knitted caps pulled down tight over their foreheads. They are unrecognizable. Liliane has never skated before but she does not dare say anything. Instead of skating in a rink, they take her to skate on a river where the ice is thick, dark and uneven and where it is windy and cold. Without a word, the two boys each take Liliane by the hand and drag her along on the ice until it is time to go back to the hotel. Liliane vows that she will never go skating again.

Every week, on Sunday, Irène makes Liliane write a letter to her father in Rome.

Chèr Papa,

Aujourd'hui, j'ai—Today, I . . . is how she begins the letter, then pauses. She does not know what to tell him. Should she write how today she went to the park and swung by herself on the baby swings and how she saw a cute little brown-and-white dog and asked the owner if she could pet him—her, the dog was female—while Irène and Gaby sat on a bench talking to each other, not paying attention to her? Or should she write how she and Miss Beecroft had supper together (frankfurters and a baked potato again), and how, as a special treat, they listened to *The Lone Ranger* on the radio and how she did not understand what was happening and Miss Beecroft had to explain? *Six Texas Rangers are ambushed by outlaws and the Lone Ranger, who is wounded, is the sole survivor. Tonto, the Apache Indian, finds him and when he recognizes that the Lone Ranger was the man who had once saved his life, he nurses him back to health. The two men dig six graves so that the outlaws will think there were no survivors. Among those killed by the outlaws is the Lone Ranger's brother and the Lone Ranger cuts a piece of cloth from his brother's black vest and, out of it, he makes a domino mask for his eyes to conceal his identity. He also vows to seek revenge for his brother's killing. Even after the outlaws are brought to justice, the Lone Ranger and Tonto continue to fight evil.*

Je t'embrasse, Liliane

She signs her name in cursive adding elaborate curlicues to the *l*s.

The following summer, Liliane is sent to camp. Camp Bueno is in New Hampshire. Before she leaves, Irène takes Liliane to a hairdresser who cuts her hair and gives her a permanent. For days after, every time Liliane catches sight of herself in a mirror or puts her hand up to touch her unfamiliar short frizzy hair, she cries.

"Short hair is more practical for camp," Irène says to comfort Liliane. "And it will dry faster when you go swimming."

"Also, it will grow," Irène adds, touching her own long blonde hair.

Camp Bueno is on a lake and the lake is full of leeches. Each time Liliane swims in it, a leech attaches itself to one of her legs or to an arm—a dangling bloated brown worm.

"If you wait a few minutes, the leech will drop off by itself," the camp counselor says.

Liliane shakes her head, she wants to scream.

"Okay then, I'll try and remove it."

The camp counselor pushes her fingernail under the leech's sucker, slides the leech off, then flicks it away quickly.

"See," she says, "that wasn't so bad."

"What if a leech gets up your nose or your ear or up your you-know-what?" Liliane asks the camp counselor.

"Then we take you to the hospital," the camp counselor answers, grinning.

Besides swimming, Liliane canoes on the lake, plays tennis, takes archery but never hits the bull's-eye, does some woodworking—she makes a box for her mother and paints a brown deer on the lid, little *Rehlein*—weaves pot holders, roasts marshmallows, and learns how to sing camp songs:

> *She'll be coming 'round the mountain when she comes,*
> *She'll be coming 'round the mountain when she comes,*
> *She'll be drivin' six white horses when she comes,*

Who will be coming around the mountain? Who will be driving six white horses? Liliane wants to know.

She hates Camp Bueno.

At the end of August, Gaby drives up in his 1948 black Ford Deluxe convertible. The top is down and Irène is sitting next to him. She has spent the summer at a dude ranch in Reno, Nevada, getting a divorce from Rudy, Liliane's father. She is wearing a red-and-white sleeveless striped dress Liliane has never seen before and she looks different—slimmer, tanner, blonder. When Irène catches sight of Liliane, she jumps out of the car and runs toward her.

"*Ma chérie,*" she calls out. "*Ma petite chérie!*"

"I have wonderful news," Irène says, kissing Liliane. "Gaby and I got married. We got married last week. I am so happy.

"*Chérie*," Irène says again, putting her tan arms around Liliane, "you'll see it will be fine. You'll be happy and I know you will like Gaby. Already, I know he loves you."

Liliane looks past Irène at Gaby. His back turned to her, he is pointing out a feature of his Ford Deluxe convertible to one of the camp counselors.

VI

Liliane never knew her two grandfathers. Waldermar, Louise's husband, died of lung cancer in Innsbruck during the Second World War. The only things she knows about him is that he was a Prussian officer and a severe disciplinarian and what she once overheard Aunt Barbara ask Irène: "Do you remember the song Papi used to sing?" and what Irène replied in a high sharp voice, "Oh, please, don't remind me. It's something I want to forget!"

> *Hoppe hoppe Reiter*
> *wenn er fälit, dann schreit er,*
> *fälit er in den Teich,*
> *find't ihn keiner gleich.*

> *Bumpety bump, rider*
> *if he falls, then he cries out,*

should he fall into the pond,
no one will find him soon.

As for Felix, Emilie's husband, who died in 1911 long before Liliane was born—apart from knowing that his name in Latin means "happiness"—Liliane has been told that he was a well-known and much admired professor of comparative linguistics at Bonn University, where he studied the grammar, phonetics, and etymology of Greek and Roman languages. Felix was killed when he was only forty-five-years old, accidentally falling out of a moving train, leaving his widow with three small children and a modest pension to live on.

Emilie does not speak of Felix and Liliane does not like to ask. However, she cannot help but speculate about the accident, trying to imagine how or why it happened. Overlooked for a prestigious chair in his department, had Felix committed suicide? Or distracted by a faculty dispute over his research—the number of occurrences, for instance, per thousand lines of enclitics in Hesiod's *Hymns?*—he lost his footing on the uneven metal couplings that join the cars? Or, and Liliane imagines a still more improbable scenario (in a photo Felix, dressed in a stiff shirt and high collar, looks stern and unapproachable), did an irate father—Felix was having an affair with a pupil, the man's daughter—stalk Felix and, while blows were being exchanged, push him off the speeding train?

What happens to Emilie and her three children during the First World War? The only clue is a sepia photo of Emilie and several other women wearing nurses' uniforms, standing among a group of German officers. No one is smiling and, staring straight at the camera, Emilie looks particularly severe. Liliane would like to imagine her grandmother as kind:

All night, instead of going home, Emilie sits by the bedside of a wounded soldier. He is seventeen years old and his Christian name is Ludwig—like Beethoven, she wants to tell him. From time to time, she puts a cold wet cloth to his face—to what is left of it. By morning, Emilie knows, Ludwig will be dead.

The occupation of the Rhineland takes place following the armistice on November 11, 1918. The occupying forces consist of American, Belgian, British, and French, and the city of Bonn lies under British jurisdiction. British soldiers are billeted in Emilie's house. Although they are civil enough, Emilie objects that the soldiers drink and smoke and put their feet up—without removing their dirty boots—on the furniture and ruin the damask chair

covers and the silk cushions. Emilie tries to hold her tongue and to keep her daughter, Edith, who is eleven and tall for her age, out of their way. She cannot be too careful, considering the growing incident of rape—although, according to rumor, the American soldiers are the worst.

The British soldiers do not leave the Rhineland until 1929, but by 1920, despite the British Commander General Sir William Robertson's worries over security, the ban against fraternization between the German population and the occupying forces has been lifted. By then, too, Emilie has gotten accustomed to and grown more tolerant of the billeted soldiers in her house. They are young and homesick, and do not mean any harm. Perhaps, too, Liliane imagines, Emilie, in spite of herself, has become fond of one of them:

A captain in the British Army, he is a bit older than the other soldiers; he has also seen and survived more battles—including two battles of Ypres, the fourth (also known as the Battle of Estaires) in the spring of 1918 and the fifth and last battle in the fall of 1918. He has been wounded and walks with a slight limp. He comes from a village in the Cotswolds—a house with a thatch roof, with hollyhocks growing in the garden, is how Emilie pictures it—where he lives with his mother. In civilian life, he is a music teacher at a boys' public school. Fortunately, the piano, a Bechstein, in Emilie's house has survived the war and Emilie urges him to make use of it. Emilie finds music to be a great solace and, each night, after the children have gone to bed, she sits in the living room and listens while he plays. He plays beautifully. Bach, especially, and Emilie is transported. . . .

But Liliane does not finish; she cannot imagine her grandmother and the British captain in bed together.

*   *   *

The 1920s in Germany are marred and marked by inflation. The inflation begins during the war, which is financed by government borrowing rather than by savings and taxation. Once Germany loses the war, it has to pay massive reparations—in addition, it has lost the economically productive Ruhr and the province of Upper Silesia—and, to do so, the government begins to print money, then more and more money, until by 1923, the government is awash with money and the money is valueless. The exchange rate between the mark and the dollar is one trillion marks to one dollar; wheelbarrows filled with money cannot buy a newspaper—it is cheaper to build a fire with banknotes than it is with a newspaper. A single egg costs Emilie 80,000,000,000 marks; a pair of shoes for Edith costs 32,000,000,000,000 marks. People barter and steal, beggars fill the streets. The inflation ends with the introduction of the Rentenmark but the blame, particularly among the middle class, who have lost all their cash savings, is laid on liberal institutions and on bankers. Some Germans go so far as to refer to the inflated banknotes as "Jew confetti." This attitude contributes to Hitler's rise to power, which coincides with his joining the Nationalsozialistische Deutsche Arbeiterpartei (National Socialist German Workers' Party, later commonly known as the Nazi Party), which is both anti-Communist and opposed to the postwar government of the Weimar Republic as well as extremely nationalistic and anti-Semitic.

On January 30, 1933, Adolf Hitler is appointed Chancellor of Germany. Four weeks later on February 27, the Reichstag goes up in flames and Hitler demands an emergency decree that restricts such democratic rights as free expression of opinion, freedom of the press, rights of assembly and intensifies security by allowing warrants for house searches and orders for confiscation of property. In less than two months Hitler has become a dictator and the transformation of Germany and the persecution of the Jews has begun in earnest. Jewish children are no longer allowed to attend public schools and have to provide for their own education. Jewish physicians are no longer allowed to practice in hospitals—or only in emergencies. Likewise, Jewish professors and teachers are deprived of their *Venia Legendi* (authorization to teach at a university), and all cultural societies have to conform with the "Aryan Clause," which again bans Jews. In addition, Jews are not allowed to buy foreign currency and permitted to send only half of their assets abroad—by 1938, that amount dwindles to only 3 percent.

Liliane's grandmother Emilie lives in Bonn but, fortunately, Fritz has a fellowship and is in Cambridge, England; Rudy, too, has left and is in Paris making films; Edith, married to a Peruvian by birth, lives on their country estate, Dunkelsdorf, located in the new German state of Schleswig-Holstein. Marguerite, Emilie's younger sister, is married to an impoverished Hungarian count and they live in Schloss Tura, an immense dilapidated castle a few miles east of Budapest; shortly before the start of the war, Marguerite's husband is rounded up by the Nazis and shot. The rest of Emilie's family live in Hamburg. A port city and a traditionally liberal one, Hamburg, Germany's window to the Anglo-Saxon world, will, for a short time, remain more tolerant in regard to its Jewish population.

In 1935, Hitler begins to prepare for war. He decrees three years of compulsory service for Germans—one in a labor force, two in the armed forces. Jews are excluded. He imposes air raid precautions—every house has to have an air warden—and gas masks are distributed to everyone but the Jews. Anti-Jewish

Helmo, the son-in-law, proves to be unreliable and, worse, he is dishonest. Officially in charge of procuring an immigration visa for his brother-in-law Rudy, Helmo, instead, does the opposite. He spreads rumors that Rudy is not to be trusted, that Rudy is a German spy. Stuck in Marseille, without a passport and without a nationality—only his French identity card—Rudy's main preoccupation, after the fall of France and once he is discharged from the Foreign Legion, is how to get out of the country. But to do so, he needs not just a passport but an exit visa, an immigration visa for Peru as well as transit visas for the different countries en route. And, as he waits to hear from Helmo, Rudy hears only of delays. In desperation, Rudy goes to the office of the American consul to try and get a visa for the United States. He explains that he has full power of attorney on an account in the Chase National Bank in New York worth $100,000, which he hopes is sufficient guarantee. For proof, Rudy cables the bank, asking them to cable back the American consul with the information.

When Rudy next sees the consul, the consul greets him coldly showing Rudy the cable from the bank which states that the account in question no longer exists. Speechless, Rudy does not know what to say or what to do next. Only much later does he understand Helmo's perfidy.

> *No other man,* he writes in his journal, *has done me so much harm or tried so hard to ruin my life than my brother-in-law . . . and never in my life had I thought that this sort of cheap melodrama could occur in our family or that I would be a part of it.*

Thanks to Josephine Baker, Rudy eventually manages to get a passport—a stateless passport—and despite Helmo's efforts to keep Rudy as far away as possible so as not to be held accountable for the money he has appropriated, a visa for Peru. From Marrakesh, Rudy goes to Casablanca, where he finds passage on a *Transat* banana boat on its way to Fort-de-France, Martinique, and from there, after a few more detours, Rudy at last arrives in Peru.

In Lima, Rudy makes friends with an American naval attaché who is also the head of U.S. Intelligence in Peru. "You know," he confides to Rudy, "before you got here, you were the most suspect of men. We had you watched in Marseille, Algeria, Casablanca, everywhere. . . ."

Does Helmo give back the $100,000? Or has he already spent it? Liliane tries to imagine their meeting. Rudy shouting at Helmo in German—calling him a *God damn Dieb* (goddamn thief), calling him a *mörder* (murderer) —or nearly one, for, if Rudy had not gotten out of France in time, he would have been rounded up with the other Jews and sent to a death camp or else perhaps, like his friend Papi Glass, simply shot in the back by a German patrol, in front of passersby on a Marseille street. And what about Rudy's sister, Edith? Whose side does she take? Despite her tears and excuses, her attempts to mediate between her husband and her brother are useless.

In the end, justice is served. Helmo's plane, a Panagra DC-3—the same type of plane Irène, Liliane, and Jeanne flew in to Peru—on its way from Arequipa to Lima, crashes into Mount Chaparra, a thirteen-thousand-foot Andean peak, killing all on board, eleven passengers and the crew of four. The probable cause, according to the accident report, was the action of the pilot in continuing the flight on instruments in the overcast. The accident was classified as the eighth worst at the time.

Edith marries again. This time she marries a Swede. Liliane has no memory of meeting Edith—she has only seen a black-and-white photograph of a slightly masculine-looking yet handsome woman—and she imagines that Edith's second husband is a kind but slightly taciturn man, who smokes a pipe and drinks aquavit. Half the year, he and Edith live in darkness, the rest in constant sunlight.

Once settled on Stewart Avenue, in Ithaca, New York, Emilie, who is not one to complain or regret the large town house in Bonn or, more recently, the pretty house in Lima with the court-yard filled with geraniums, keeps busy. She maintains a huge correspondence, typing letters on her German typewriter that has an *o* with an umlaut, to family members—to the ones who managed to survive by fleeing to England—to friends left behind in Peru, to her son Rudy, in Rome, who dutifully answers her every Sunday, and to her only grandchild, Liliane, in New York City, who seldom writes back.

Instead, on her school holidays, Liliane visits Emilie in Ithaca and, as usual, while they walk together, Emilie continues telling Liliane stories.

"Remember how I told you that your great-grandfather Rudolf Brach arrived in New Orleans on November 26, 1848, and met Joseph Hernsheim, his uncle?"

Taking Emilie's arm, Liliane nods, "The uncle gave him fifty dollars."

"And I told you how his uncle was in the business of ready-made cotton clothing and that he made Rudolf a partner," Emilie continues.

"And how Rudolf goes to Mexico," Liliane says.

"Yes," Emilie says before launching once more into her story, "and after five stormy days on a schooner called the *Shannon*, Rudolf reaches Brazos Santiago on the Gulf of Mexico; from there he takes a smaller boat to Port Isabel, then a mule cart to Brownsville, Texas. Along the way, he describes how the countryside is filled with small, gnarly, crippled mesquite trees and prickly cactus shrubs and how all the vegetation is full of thorns, even the grass has edges like a saw.

"Brownsville is built like a camp; the huts and tents have almost no furniture and Rudolf has to sleep on the ground. To make matters worse, the town is experiencing a cholera epidemic. Hundreds of people die. In the streets, the corpses are placed into wheelbarrows then thrown in the river—the river water that the townspeople drink—or in the woods for the vultures, who gather in flocks of thousands."

"Is that true?" Liliane asks, frowning.

Emilie nods but does not answer, "Most of the townspeople are thieves. Their chief possessions are pistols and knives and they make their living by stealing horses and cheating at card games. The best thing that can be said about them is that they often shoot one another—"

Liliane laughs.

"Rudolf, too, has to carry a pistol and learn how to use it. He also has to learn how to ride a horse, his principal means of transportation. But let me go on—from Brownsville, Rudolf follows the Rio Grande upriver, along the Mexican border."

"How old was Rudolf?" Liliane interrupts. "I forget."

"I told you, he was nineteen—just a few years older than you," Emilie answers. "Traveling with him are three Mexicans. At villages along the way, Rudolf sells his wares: cloth, sewing cotton, knives, axes, shovels, coffee, sugar. The land he rides through is made up of vast prairies with thousands of wild horses and marauding Comanche and Apache tribes. The Indians are particularly feared as they plunder and burn villages, kill the men and take the women and children."

"Did Rudolf meet any Indians?" Liliane starts to ask.

"Yes, on another trip, a woman and the two men in Rudolf's party go ahead, and when Rudolf and the rest of his party catch up to them, they find that the two men and the woman have been shot by Indians. The two men are dead and the woman has a terrible gash in her chest but has survived. Just as they are trying to help her the Indians return, and Rudolf and his party have to leave her to seek cover behind the wagons. The attack is repelled but when they go back to where the woman was lying, she is dead."

"Who was she?" Liliane asks.

"Stagecoach robbers were also a problem," Emilie continues. "Another time, while Rudolf is waiting to take a stagecoach from Guanajuato to Aguascalientes, the stagecoach is late. Due to arrive in Guanajuato at four, it is five, then it is six o'clock, and still no sign of the stagecoach. The people waiting for their relatives or waiting for newspapers and mail become more and more concerned and just as they are getting ready to send an express rider to investigate, they hear the crack of the whip and the stagecoach appears at a canter. Everyone rushes to the stagecoach to learn the cause of the delay but they are immediately told to stand back. Apparently, the stagecoach was robbed. Robbed twice. The second time—since there was so little left to rob—the bandits took all the passengers' clothes." Emilie pauses a moment.

"And there were two ladies among the passengers. Shall we sit down for a minute," Emilie also says.

At a bus stop, on a bench, Emilie and Liliane rest for a while and Liliane asks, "How do you know so much about Rudolf? Did he tell you those stories?"

"In the evening after dinner, if he was in a good humor, he told us children about his adventures. He also kept a journal. My father was not an easy man but he was an honest one and his intentions were good," Emilie answers.

In my early days, the reason my aspirations centered mainly on the acquisition of so-called worldly goods is to be found in the fact that I had seen the battle with the wolf at the door from too close quarters in my childhood and that I was thus led in this direction from the start. Perhaps in so doing, I ought to have been less neglectful of more idealistic endeavors, perhaps I should have placed myself between two chairs.

Emilie goes on. "Rudolf spent nearly thirteen years in North America and the reason he left was the impending Civil War. The ports were closed and it would be difficult to transport goods. But by then he had built up a big export business from Hamburg, Paris, and Manchester to Monterrey, Mexico, and by then, too, he had made quite a fortune." Emilie smiles. "Rudolf's capital grew from eight-thousand dollars in 1853 to three-hundred-thousand in 1858. He also owned a three-thousand-square-mile estate in Mexico, which included a farm for breeding bulls, a cotton and sugar plantation, and a hat factory. A pity he didn't keep it," Emile adds. "We could have all gone to Mexico during the war instead of to Peru."

In 1866 Rudolf married Fides (short for Friederike, née Feist Belmont) and in 1868 he went back to Mexico. He did not return to Paris, where his wife and children were then living—in a house Victor Hugo later bought but never paid them for— until 1870, right before the start of the Franco-Prussian War and right after the birth of his daughter Emilie. As a child, Emilie remembered being intimidated by Rudolf. He appeared distant and disinterested in his daughters (there were to be three) and Emilie could not help but feel that she, as the second born and another girl, was a great disappointment to him. On learning of her birth, he wrote from America to Fides:

> We have a second daughter and have to be satisfied with our fate. . . . The result of it is that with two female descendants I must exert myself more than ever in order to earn something and to provide for them. I must renounce all sentimentality and inclination for easy living and I must in this stern world try to capture for my daughters the livelihood that is due to them.

Nor was Fides known to be especially warmhearted or maternal. She drove her children hard, making them study and learn their lessons by heart. In fact, Rudolf already had had a glimpse of this quality when he first went to court her: on his arrival at her house in Alzey, his horse shied suddenly, throwing Rudolf off, and Fides, who was looking out the window, laughed. Rudolf got back on his horse and rode off, vowing, at the time, never to see Fides again as he thought her "hard-hearted."

* * *

Standing up, Emilie tells Liliane, "Shall we keep walking? And I just remembered something else. On his way back to Germany in 1861, Rudolf happens to stop off in Washington on the very day of the presidential inauguration. He manages to get inside the White House and, although Rudolf's sympathies lie with the South, he has the good fortune to meet Abraham Lincoln."

"Is this true?" Liliane asks again.

"Congratulations, Mr. President," always polite, Rudolf says, taking Abraham Lincoln's hand.

"Thank you, sir," equally polite, Abraham Lincoln replies, shaking Rudolf's hand. Detecting a slight foreign accent, he also asks, "Whereabouts are you from, sir?"

"Germany, from the Rhineland. You must come and visit us one day, Mr. President. The countryside is very beautiful and we make excellent wine."

"Yes, one day, I would like to visit your country," Abraham Lincoln answers. "God willing, if we do not go to war," he adds.

VII

Her eyes open, Liliane is sitting up in bed screaming.

"*Chérie, chérie,* what is it?" Wearing only a sheer silk nightgown, Irène tries to calm her.

Liliane does not seem to hear her. When Irène puts her arms around her, Liliane roughly pushes her away.

"Get me a washcloth with cold water," Irène tells Gaby, who is standing at the bedroom door. Instead of pajamas, he wears boxer shorts.

"Jesus!" he says. "What's going on? She woke me up."

"Please, a cold washcloth," Irène repeats.

When she tries to apply the cold washcloth to Liliane's face, Liliane slaps away Irène's hand and stands up. Jumping up and down on the bed, she continues to scream.

More than a nightmare, what Liliane experiences is closer in intensity to what is known as an incubus attack or *pavor nocturnus.* These night terrors occur in children between the ages of four and twelve and usually disappear during adolescence. Symptoms include sweating, rapid respiration and heart rate, thrashing of limbs such as punching and hitting, and screaming. The child may appear to be awake but he or she will also be inconsolable and unresponsive to efforts to communicate with him or her and also may not recognize those familiar attempting to do so. Chances are, too, the child will be unable to describe the dream.

For the next few years, Liliane will continue to experience night terrors and have the same recurring dream. The dream has to do with numbers. An infinite set of numbers.

In school, Liliane is good at math—algebra, geometry, calculus are a breeze. In fact, once she has mastered the English language, she does well in all subjects—she is an A student. At commencement, she gets prizes: one year, the complete works of Robert Frost for the highest average in examinations in the upper school; another year, the complete works of T. S. Eliot for the highest average in daily work in the upper school. She acts in school plays (Brutus in *Julius Caesar,* Myrtle Webb in *Our Town,* Black Dog in *Treasure Island*), she is president of the Lit Club and co-editor of the yearbook. In addition, she is on the volleyball and basketball teams—one of her long shots determines the winning score of a crucial game.

She also makes friends: Mary Lou Harvey, Jane Mackintosh, Alice Zimmer (Zimmy for short), Marion (Mimi) Holbrook, Sarah Cohen, and her best friend—now that Margo Maximov has moved to Philadelphia—Pamela Wylie. Pamela wants to be a poet and her poems—poems heavily influenced by the work of

e. e. cummings—are published regularly in the school magazine under a single moniker, which she pronounces *Pa-MAY-LA,* accenting the last two syllables. One of her poems goes like this:

> *i skip past the evening sky*
> *past the boughs of trees*
> *fat green fingers reaching for*
> *the clouds*
> *the dinner bell rings*
> *And i skip home*

Pamela lives a few blocks from Liliane and, often, instead of going home from school right away, Liliane goes to Pamela's apartment. There, they drink Cokes laced with rum and smoke cigarettes—Pamela's mother is either out or too inebriated to notice or care. Janice, Pamela's pretty younger sister, however, does care and complains that the smoke makes it hard for her to breathe. Janice suffers from asthma. Poor Janice.

Poor Janice, indeed. On August 28, 1963, Janice Wylie and her roommate, Emily Hoffert, are brutally murdered in their Upper East Side apartment. Both girls are stabbed more than sixty times with kitchen knives and Janice, who apparently had just stepped out of the shower wrapped in a towel, is found nude. She has been sexually assaulted as well as eviscerated— her intestines are lying on the floor next to her. The killings are dubbed the "Career Girls Murders" by the media because Janice, who works as a *Newsweek* researcher, is the niece of the writer Philip Wylie and Emily, an elementary-school teacher, is one of the thousands of young women who have come from all over the United States to New York City seeking a job. Hundreds of detectives are assigned to the case and the story is front-page news for months.

George Whitmore, a nineteen-year-old, unemployed African American with an IQ below 100, is wrongfully accused of the crime. His confession, it turns out, was coerced by the police. He is imprisoned for over two years, released on bond for nearly six years, and is finally exonerated in 1973. His treatment by the negligent and possibly racist police force plays a significant role in the U.S. Supreme Court's decision to issue the guidelines for future police interrogations known as the Miranda rights. In addition, his particular case leads to the abolishment of the New York State death penalty. The real killer, Richard Robles, a twenty-two-year-old heroin addict, is arrested on January 26, 1965, and confesses to the murders, saying: "I went to pull a lousy burglary and I wound up killing two girls." He is sentenced to life imprisonment; his repeated requests for parole are denied.

Pamela, the poet, dies young as well; her death, the result of untreated Legionnaires' disease, goes unnoticed.

At age seven, Liliane nearly dies of diphtheria. As a disease, diphtheria has been nearly eradicated in industrialized nations by the DPT (diphtheria-pertussin-tetanus) vaccine. However before 1920, there were an estimated 200,000 cases of diphtheria annually in the United States, causing 15,000 deaths per year. The most famous outbreak occurred in 1925 in Nome, Alaska, which led to a serum run known as the "Great Race of Mercy," where twenty mushers and more than one hundred dogs relayed diphtheria antitoxin by sled across Alaska for five and a half days over a distance of 674 grueling miles, thus saving the city of

Nome from a deadly epidemic. A statue in New York City's Central Park commemorates the lead dog, Balto, who arrived with the twenty-pound serum-filled cylinder in Nome on February 2 at 5:30 a.m. However, another dog, Togo, is considered the true hero as he covered the most hazardous stretch of the journey and carried the serum longer—91 miles, to Balto's 53 miles.

The year is 1947 and Liliane and Irène are spending the summer in the French Alps. They are staying at a small hotel. The hotel is owned by a Monsieur Gruass. At mealtimes, Monsieur Gruass manages the hotel dining room and is overly punctilious. Everyone dislikes him. During lunch one day, to annoy him and to show off, Liliane says: "Monsieur Gruyère, may I have some Gruass?" That same afternoon, while she is playing "doctor" with the other children staying at the hotel, Liliane, who is the "patient," starts to feel sick. Really sick. A punishment for her rudeness to Monsieur Gruass, she assumes. Too soon after the war, the hospital in Chamonix is small, underequipped, and staffed with nuns. No antitoxin vaccine for diphtheria is available. During the first few days, her throat closed, unable to breathe properly, with a fever of 40.6 degrees Celsius (105 degrees Fahrenheit), Liliane's life hangs in the balance.

Irène leaves her only to get something to drink (she cannot think about food) or to try to telephone Rudy, who has stayed behind in Paris. The telephone is located in the hospital emergency waiting room and is unreliable—long-distance calls have to be placed in advance and are expensive—and, anyway, Irène is apprehensive. She and Rudy are about to separate and barely speak to each other or, if they do, they shout. When Irène finally reaches Rudy—again, on account of the bad connection, she has to shout—she has to tell him that Liliane is gravely ill and might . . . although she cannot bring herself to say the word.

"Her fever . . . ," Irène starts to say.

"What about Liliane? I can barely hear you."

"I said she has a very high fever," Irène repeats.

"Where is she?"

"The hospital is small but the nuns are competent."

"She can't stay in Chamonix," Rudy shouts back. "You must bring her to Paris immediately."

"She is in quarantine—"

The line goes dead.

While Irène tries to call Rudy back, the door to the hospital opens and a stretcher is brought in. The boy on the stretcher appears to be seventeen or eighteen years old; his face is smooth, unblemished. His blond hair sticks to his forehead and looks wet; he has on a dark blue windbreaker, and except for one booted foot that hangs over the stretcher at an unnatural angle, his body is covered with a blanket. A doctor, followed by a nun, comes running into the emergency waiting room. The doctor takes one of the boy's hands in his, feels for his pulse, then, very gently, he lets the hand go.

Irène hangs up the receiver and asks, "Is he dead?"

She watches as the nun pulls up the blanket to cover the boy's face.

"A mountain climbing accident," the nun tells her, sighing. "On the Aiguille du Midi. It happens every summer."

The reason Irène and Liliane are spending the summer in the French Alps is Claude. Claude and Irène first met in Lisbon, in 1940. During the war, Portugal had maintained its neutrality

and was relatively safe—Antonio Salazar, the dictatorial prime minister, played a game of fence-sitting between the Allies and the Axis—and safe as long as one had not been refused or arrested at the border and had the prerequisite papers. In Irène's case, she had the entry visa for Portugal and she was waiting for a transit visa to the United States (eventually, she obtained one for three days) and for another to Peru. Liliane, Jeanne, and Irène were staying at the Palácio Estoril, an elegant hotel situated on the coast, a dozen miles from Lisbon. The hotel had a casino, a golf course, tennis courts, and a pool, and was home to royals, spies, and double agents—including Dusko Popov, one of the most famous or infamous, who was said to be the model for James Bond. While Irène waited, she swam, sunbathed, and gambled.

Meanwhile, Claude and his cousin, Charles, answering General de Gaulle's call to all Frenchmen to join him in Britain, were on their way from Oran, Algeria, via Gibraltar, to St. Athan, a pilot training center in Wales, when their plane made an unscheduled stop in Lisbon. The reason for this, the men on board were told, was that their commanding officer had arranged a secret meeting with the Portuguese minister of defense—only, to Charles, Claude joked that the secret meeting was probably with a woman. Everyone was told to wait until the next day or perhaps even the day after for the flight to England to resume. Claude and Charles found a room in a cheap hotel in the city center, washed up, had drinks, dinner, then made their way by taxi to the casino at the Palácio Estoril.

Irène was playing roulette. Very tanned from sunbathing by the pool, she wore a white silk dress and her blonde hair was swept back by a sparkling comb.

She was losing.

"*À cheval*," she told the croupier, placing six chips on the pairs 0–3, 1–4, 2–5, 3–6, 7–8, 8–9.

The ball landed on 14.

"*À cheval*," Irène said again, placing her last six chips on 0–1, 1–2, 2–3, 4–5, 5–6.

The ball landed on 32.

Sitting down next to her, Claude placed a stack of chips in front of Irène.

"What's your favorite number?" he asked her.

"Seven," Irène answered

Claude placed all the chips on numbers 7, 17, and 27.

"*Finales en plein*," he told the croupier.

The ball landed on 27. The payout was 35 to 3.

"Let's go. We don't have much time," Claude said to Irène, as he pocketed the chips and waved good-bye to Charles.

Claude, the love of Irène's life—romantic, dashing, impetuous, charming, lucky, sexy Claude!

Married, Claude, from the start, has told Irène that he can never leave his wife. His wife is the daughter of a wealthy French banking family. One would never guess that Jacqueline is heir to one of the richest fortunes in France—she dresses simply and, except for her wedding ring, wears almost no jewelry. Nor is Jacqueline what the French call *mondaine*—social. She is a professor of literature at the Sorbonne and good friends with Jean-Paul Sartre, Simone de Beauvoir—Simone especially—and Nathalie Sarraute.

In the Planpraz cable car, on their way up to hike the Col du Brévent, Claude tells Irène, "I remember when they built it. 1928. The same year my family bought the chalet."

"And you've come to Chamonix ever since?" Irène asks.

Instead of answering, Claude says, "It's the highest cable car in the world and a great feat of engineering, but Jacqueline won't ride in it."

"How did you meet?" Irène asks.

"In school."

"The Lycée Janson?"

"Of course," Claude replies.

Then he adds, "Do you know the story of the lycée?"

Claude likes to tell stories.

Irène shakes her head. "Only that it is the most prestigious high school in France and that Jean Gabin and Roland Garros went there as students."

"Monsieur Janson de Sailly was a very rich man, a lawyer, but, one day, to his immense chagrin, he discovered that his beloved wife was being unfaithful to him."

"What did he do?" Irène makes a face. "Kill her?"

"Worse," Claude says. "He disinherited her and left all his money to the state on condition that it establish a modern high school that offered an excellent education—the Lycée Janson turned out to be the first public school in France. Monsieur Janson made another condition," Claude continues with a smile, "that women were not permitted in the lycée."

Halfway up Le Brévent, he and Irène sit down on a secluded grassy spot, in the sun, off the hiking trail. Nearby, in the shade, are patches of dirty snow. They have stopped to eat lunch—bread, cheese, salami; they also have wine, a black market bottle of Swiss Fendant. Below them lies a small alpine lake, Lac Blanc, and beyond them rise the snow-covered Mont Blanc and the Aiguille du Midi.

"Every summer, Charles and I used to climb the Aiguille du Midi," Claude tells Irène. "Poor Charles. I miss him. His plane was hit over Saint-Omer in the Pas-de-Calais."

"You saw it?" Irène asks.

Stationed south of London at Biggin Hill during the war, Claude flew missions over France and Belgium. Often, on a clear day, he would catch a glimpse of his native country below—the Eiffel Tower once, the River Seine, winding through the countryside like a silver ribbon. He flew a Spitfire IX, equipped with a Rolls-Royce Merlin 63 engine and two-stage superchargers. The superchargers were a lifesaver, although it took two minutes—two minutes that felt to him like two years—before the blower was activated and before Claude was out of range from enemy fire. But Claude was lucky. Modest, too, he rarely speaks of his exploits—how often he came close to being killed, how often he saw friends and enemies both killed.

And always his cousin, Charles. Over and over, Claude cannot help but relive in his mind's eye the sight of Charles's plane as the fuel tank is hit, and as it begins its spiral descent earthward, spewing black smoke, and how a small dark shape detaches itself from the cockpit, falls with the smoking plane, and, as the parachute opens, floats free of it. Then, no matter how much Claude hopes against hope, the inevitable always happens—a spark from the falling plane, the parachute catches fire, and, in an instant, is consumed. Over the Channel, that day, on Claude's way back to Biggin Hill, the sky was a startling and unrelenting blue and, without a cloud cover, he flew at 30,000 feet to avoid detection. In pure oxygen, it was hard-going and cold—the outside temperature was minus 50 degrees, inside the cockpit minus 25 degrees—and the tears flowing down Claude's cheeks froze.

"You would have liked Charles," Claude says after a while, smiling. Claude's smile is what first drew Irène. Claude is handsome in an easy, relaxed way for which the French have a saying: *se sentir bien dans sa peau,* which means "feeling comfortable in one's skin."

"One day, I'll take you up there," Claude says, pointing with his chin to the Aiguille du Midi.

"I'll teach you how to rock climb."

"I'd like that," Irène says.

The stony path ascends steeply, beyond the tree line and past twisted scrub vegetation; they cross a moraine of rocks, then a little stream of melted snow. Claude holds out his hand to Irène and although she takes it, she says, "I am fine."

When they reach a fixed metal ladder on a rock wall, Claude lets Irène go up first.

"In case you fall, I'll catch you," he tells her.

"I won't fall," Irène answers. She wants to show Claude that she is not afraid.

Irène is wearing shorts and, looking up at her calf muscles flexing right above his head, Claude starts to get an erection.

At the top, Irène, as an afterthought, asks, "But didn't Jacqueline go to the Lycée Janson?"

"Fortunately, a few years later, the lycée allowed girls," Claude says.

"We should start back," Irène says then, "or Liliane will worry."

* * *

Growing up, Liliane does not spend a lot of time with Gaby. He works on Wall Street, investing other people's money, and he comes home late. Immediately on opening the front door and taking off his coat, he goes to the little table in the living room that is set up as a bar and mixes himself a bourbon and water.

"Irène!" From her bedroom, Liliane hears him calling. "Where's the ice?"

"There's no ice in the ice bucket," he repeats. "Why is it that every night when I come home—"

"I know, I know. I've told Helena a million times," Irène says, as she comes running down the hall. "She always forgets."

During dinner, Gaby drinks a second or perhaps it is a third bourbon and water, Irène drinks a glass of wine, and Liliane drinks nothing at all. After they have finished their soup, Helena, the cook, places their meal—lamb chops, creamed spinach, and roast potatoes—on top of the sideboard on a hot plate so the food won't get cold.

Getting up, Irène asks Gaby, "One or two lamb chops?"

"One," Gaby answers. He eats little.

"And what about spinach and potatoes? The potatoes look delicious," Irène says, putting both vegetables on his plate.

"That's too much," Gaby says, taking another drink of his bourbon and water.

Irène shrugs. "It's good for you."

"Please don't tell me what is good for me."

Liliane helps herself to only the spinach.

"*Chérie!*" Irène says to her. "Is that all you're going to eat?"

"I'm not hungry," Liliane answers, looking down at her plate.

* * *

In an effort to befriend her, Gaby offers Liliane one dollar a week if she will shine his shoes—a whole array of them in his closet: black, brown, lace-up oxfords, loafers, boots. He shows her how.

"First, you pull out the laces," he tells her, "then you take this brush and brush off the dirt, especially around the soles. After you've done that, you take a rag and dip it into the shoe polish—black or brown, depending—and cover the shoe with polish. And don't forget the tongue. Now, if you want to get a really high polish—a spit polish"—Gaby is holding up one of his shoes to show Liliane—"don't worry, you don't have to spit," he says, trying to make it a joke. "Soldiers spit if there is no water around but we have plenty of water. Then, using the rag again, you mix the polish with water, just a little like this, and you rub it on the shoe again. You rub and rub"—again, Gaby stops to show Liliane—"until you get a high shine. Do you understand, Lillian?"

Liliane nods.

But she cannot thread the laces the way Gaby has shown her—the zigzag "ladder lacing" he learned in the navy—and, one time, not paying attention, she puts brown polish on a black shoe. Worse, she cannot achieve the high polish Gaby has in mind.

"It's okay, Lillian," Gaby tells Liliane, after a few days. "I'll polish them myself. But, here," he adds, handing her a dollar, "this is for trying."

Often, after dinner, while Liliane is in her room doing her homework, she can hear Irène and Gaby begin to argue. She tries not to listen to what they are saying but their voices carry.

I told you that we had to go out for dinner. They are important clients.

You didn't tell me.

I told you last week.

You never told me.

Don't argue with me, Irène. Gaby's voice becomes louder, angrier.

So does Irène's. *You never told me!*

I did so tell you, damn it!

Very often, the door to Irène's bedroom slams shut. Then there is silence and Liliane goes back to her homework:

$2(3x - 7) + 4(3x + 2) = 6(5x + 9) + 3$

During the war, Gaby was in the U.S. Navy; he was a lieutenant. He was stationed in London and on the way over, his ship, the USS *Ingraham*, escorting convoys between the United States, Iceland, and the United Kingdom and carrying much needed supplies to the Allies, collided with the oil tanker *Chemung* in thick fog off the coast of Nova Scotia. The depth charges in the ship's stern exploded and the *Ingraham* sank. Gaby and a half dozen other men were able to climb into a lifeboat and survive the collision. But due to the fog and the rough seas, they were not rescued for thirty-six hours and by then, they were wet, cold, and suffering from hypothermia.

"Were you frightened?" Liliane is not sure what to say.

"I tried to stay warm and to stay sane. One of the men in the lifeboat took off all his clothes and threw them overboard."

"Why?" Liliane asks.

"Apparently the muscles contracting blood vessels relax in extreme cold weather and cause blood to flow to the extremities, tricking the person into believing he is hot." Gaby adds, "Or so I have been told."

"And did the man die?" Liliane persists.

Gaby doesn't answer right away. Then he says, "Lillian, I'd rather talk about something else."

When he finally got to London, Gaby joined the headquarters for General Dwight D. Eisenhower under Admiral Harold R. Stark, the commander of naval forces in Europe. "Known as Betty," Gaby tells Liliane. "Only we did not call him that to his face. Poor fellow, he was blamed for not sharing intelligence about Pearl Harbor, but he turned out to be a real hero—with three navy and one army Distinguished Service Medals for his part in D-Day."

Irène is in Tanganyika, visiting her sister, Uli, for two weeks, and, except for Helena, the cook, who may have gone out or gone to bed already, Gaby and Liliane are alone in the apartment, after dinner.

"Stark was responsible for overseeing the naval buildup for the invasion," Gaby continues. With Irène away, Gaby seems more relaxed and less combative and Liliane, who is studying World War II in school, wants to take advantage of his good humor and ask him questions.

"What did you do? Were you busy gathering secret intelligence?" She is half joking, half serious.

"No, nothing like that," Gaby answers. "Mostly, I shuffled papers in an office, but I have to admit—despite what was going on, the war and all—I had a hell of a good time in London."

Liliane frowns slightly. "Where did you live?"

"At Brown's. The hotel was full of characters, like in a novel," Gaby gives a laugh. "Including Winston Churchill, who came to Brown's regularly after work for a drink. I can still see him sitting hunched over at the bar and I remember the bartender, too . . . what was his name? Damn, I know it as well as my own." Gaby pauses to take another sip of his drink. "But you, miss, with your nose buried in a book all day, might appreciate this—Rudyard Kipling wrote *The Jungle Book* at Brown's. There were other writers who stayed there, too, but I forget who. Anyway, everyone stays at Brown's. Either at Brown's or at Claridge's," Gaby says.

"And there were plenty of nightclubs with great music and dancing," Gaby adds.

"Did you dance?" Liliane asks.

A few times, when everyone is out and Liliane is alone in the apartment, she takes out Gaby's navy uniform, which is wrapped in plastic and hangs in the back of his closet—a smart double-breasted blue jacket with two gold stripes and a star on the sleeves and shiny copper buttons and matching navy pants—and examines it. Once, she goes through the pockets but finds nothing; another time she tries on the jacket. Wearing it, she stands in front of the closet mirror and, saluting herself, she does a little jig.

No doubt, Gaby, as a young man, cut a handsome figure in his uniform. Although short—in heels, Irène stands taller—he is good-looking in a compact, robust way; in college, he boxed competitively and won his bouts. Liliane can picture him walking in fashionable Mayfair, wearing his white officer's cap and saluting left and right to stylish ladies—Fiona, Clarissa, Edwina.

"Who was Edwina?" Suddenly curious, Liliane asks.

"Lady Edwina." Gaby leans back in his chair and lights a Cuban cigar—a forbidden cigar, because Irène claims the smell gives her a migraine. "She was quite a girl, that Edwina."

Smiling, Gaby starts to reminisce. "She was a looker, too—not as good-looking as your mother, but still . . ."

Liliane pictures Gaby and a dark-haired, slender Edwina dancing cheek to cheek to a quick fox-trot in the dim basement of a nightclub, ignoring the air raid sirens, then ignoring the falling bombs.

"I didn't get to London until 1943 and, by then, the Blitz was over," Gaby says, nearly reading Liliane's mind, "and it was not until the following year that the Germans began attacking again. Then it was almost worse because they used V-weapons or flying pilotless bombs. It took the missiles five minutes to get to London from Germany or from Belgium, where they were launched, and radar wasn't quick enough to pick them up. And you couldn't hear them coming. You only heard the sonic boom after the blast. Thousands of Brits were killed or injured." Gaby pauses a moment. "Edwina was one of them. She had just come out of Selfridge's, where she had gone Christmas shopping, and one of the bombs fell as she was crossing Duke Street."

"I'm sorry," Liliane says.

"I am, too," Gaby says. "She was a great gal."

"Edwina had her dog with her," Gaby says after a while. "A little black cairn. The cairn survived."

"What happened to him?" Liliane asks.

"Her. I took her for a while—until I could find a proper home for her. A little rascal. She made my life hell." Gaby laughs. "She bit the chambermaid, she chewed my one good pair of Lobb shoes. Her name was Winnie. Named after either Churchill or Winnie the Pooh. Or both." Again, Gaby laughs.

Liliane, too, laughs.

"But maybe I am boring you with all this?" Gaby says. "My wartime exploits."

"No." Liliane says. "I like hearing about them."

"My exploits," Gaby repeats softly, shaking his head, before he takes another puff of his Cuban cigar.

"Donald," Gaby says all of a sudden. "I just remembered. Donald—the name of the bartender. He was Irish."

Did you meet Winston Churchill? Liliane wants to ask, but does not. *Did you have drinks with him at the hotel bar?*

And Claude—did you meet him?

VIII

A summer morning in Rome, too hot, from sunbathing on the terrace, and Maria is out marketing, Liliane, with nothing better to do and not sure what she is looking for, goes to her father's desk and starts to riffle through the drawers. She finds letters—letters from Emilie, her grandmother (those are easy to recognize because Emilie types them on her old German typewriter), letters from Fritz, whose handwriting is small and nearly illegible, letters from Irène, whose writing Liliane knows well, and letters from women, she guesses, she does not know, all neatly stacked together. Jammed in the back of one of the drawers, she also finds a book, *Histoire d'O*, and, lying next to it, the key chain with the four-leaf clover charm she gave her father one Christmas years ago.

Sitting at her father's desk, still dressed in only her bathing suit, Liliane puts aside the letters and begins to read *Histoire d'O*.

Deux mains soulevèrent sa cape, deux autres descendaient
le long de ses reins après avoir vérifié l'attache des bracelets:
elles n'étaient pas gantées, et l'une la pénétra de deux parts à
la fois, si bruquement qu'elle cria. Quelqu'un rit. Quelqu'un
d'autre dit: "Retournez-la, qu'on voie les seins et le ventre."
On la fit tourner. . . .

(Two hands lifted her cape, two others—after having checked
to see that her bracelets were attached—descended the length
of her back and buttocks. The hands were not gloved, and
one of them penetrated her in both places at once, so abruptly
that she cried out. Someone laughed. Someone else said:
"Turn her around, so we can see the breasts and belly." They
turned her around. . . .)

That year Liliane's father's mistress is Francine; she is colored and from Jamaica.

The summer before it was Claudia. A brunette, Claudia wore her thick hair in a single French braid. Obsessed with Claudia's braid, Liliane spent hours in front of the mirror trying to plait her fine hair into one like Claudia's. Portuguese, Claudia sang *fado*—heartbreaking songs of romantic disillusionment and longing. One evening, Rudy drove Liliane in the silver Lancia to *Belvedere delle Rose,* a popular outdoor nightclub outside of Rome, to hear Claudia sing. What impressed Liliane most about the evening was not Claudia's singing but the act that followed hers, a striptease, and how at the last possible moment when the stripper leaned over to take off her top, *she* turned out to be a man.

In her early twenties, Francine is both glamorous and friendly. She once had a role playing a slave in *Quo Vadis.* She described how, nearly naked, she was made to stand for hours holding two tame cheetahs on a leash—only, according to Francine, the cheetahs were not tame—while the scene was shot over and over again and how, finally, the scene was cut from the film. Until now, Liliane had never met a colored person—there are no colored girls in her private school and Gaby and Irène have no colored friends. Walking down the Via Veneto with Francine, everyone looks at them. Not just the men; the women, too, look. And although Liliane knows that the looks are not directed at her (except now that she is older Italian men do look at her and call out, *Bambola*—doll), she feels special. She is proud to be in Francine's company.

"What part of Jamaica are you from?" Liliane asks her.

"Mandeville? Do you know it?"

Liliane shakes her head.

"Mandeville is not on the coast but inland, on a plateau. It's quite different from the rest of Jamaica. If you were to go there, you'd think you were in an English village. There's a town green, a church, a courthouse, a library, and all the names are English: Battersea, Knockpatrick, Clover, Waltham—" Francine gives a laugh. "The weather, too, is different," Francine continues. "It's cooler."

"And your parents?" Liliane asks.

"My mother works as a maid in a hotel and my father has part-time jobs, but mostly he drinks. Before that, my grandparents worked on a sugar plantation—but now the plantations are all gone."

"Why?" Liliane asks.

Francine shrugs. "The price of sugar went way down. Instead, they grow bananas." Again, she laughs.

"And why did you leave Jamaica?"

"As a teenager—I was about your age, maybe a little older—I was bored and I did not want to go to school so I would hitch a ride to the beach at Negril and one day a famous French photographer saw me and took my picture. He told me I could be a model. I believed him and I left Jamaica."

"Would you go back?"

"All these questions," Francine says. After pausing a moment, she says, "There's an old Jamaican saying that goes, Talk and taste your tongue, which means think before you speak. I know you mean well and that you are a nice intelligent girl but, to tell the truth, talking about Jamaica breaks my heart."

That same summer Liliane reads Françoise Sagan's novel *Bonjour Tristesse* and, in part, identifies with it. But unlike the narrator, Cecile, who plots to get rid of her father's mistress and inadvertently causes her death, Liliane, early on, recognizes the advantages of her situation. Liliane knows no one her own age in Rome—even if she did, most Italian teenagers, she guesses, would have left the city for Porto Ercole or Forte di Marme—and she must turn to Francine (and to the other young women in her father's life—and there are many) for companionship, for friendship even. More important, the young women make it easier for Liliane to be with her father. She is no longer the sole object of his attention or of his affection—affection not always apparent to Liliane.

But Rudy is generous—generous to a fault. Money is there to be spent, not saved, and once a week, he takes out his gold money clip, peels off huge bills—one-hundred-thousand-lire bills—and hands them to Liliane. He does not ask her how she spends it, in the same spirit, perhaps, that he does not attempt to explain his relationships. Rudy makes no embarrassing confessions or uses any subterfuges; instead, he is discreet. Liliane has not heard any compromising sounds nor seen her father in an inappropriate position; she has never seen him do anything more amorous than kiss a woman on the cheek. In the evening, after dinner, he drives Liliane home, then he takes Francine home. Most nights, Liliane is asleep by the time Rudy returns to the apartment off Via Salaria and he is always home the next morning.

In *Bonjour Tristesse*, Cecile's father behaves exactly like Rudy:

Quand nous rentrions, mon père me déposait et le plus souvent allait reconduire une amie. Je ne l'entendais pas rentrer.

Je ne veux pas laisser croire qu'il mît une ostentation quelconque à ses aventures. Il se bornait à ne pas me les cacher, plus exactement à ne rien me dire de convenable et de faux. . . .

(At the end of the evening my father would drop me at our flat, and then see his companion home. I never heard him come in.

I do not want to give the impression that he was vain about his love affairs, but he made no effort to hide them from me, or to invent stories or to explain. . . .)

Nevertheless, at breakfast, Liliane looks for a sign of the previous night's sex on her father's face—a bruise, a swollen lip—even though she has a hard time picturing him making love and in bed with Francine. His hairy belly against her dark flat one? His blue-veined legs around her smooth black back? Or his balding head pressed in between her long slender legs? *Histoire d'O* has opened Liliane's eyes to unknown and disturbing lovemaking possibilities—lovemaking possibilities that Liliane, up until now had known nothing about.

> *Quand il la lâcha, gémissante et salie de larmes sous son bandeau, elle glissa à terre: ce fut pour sentir des genoux contre son visage, et que sa bouche ne serait pas épargnée.*

> *(When he let her go, sobbing and befouled by tears beneath her blindfold, she slipped to the floor, only to feel someone's knees against her face, and she realized that her mouth was not to be spared.)*

"Pass me the cheese, please," Rudy tells Liliane as he spreads butter on his bread, his appetite unaffected by the amorous exploits of the night before.

Then, Rudy goes back to reading the newspaper.

Several months earlier, a Reuters correspondent present at the historic signing of the Treaty of Rome (by France, West Germany, Italy, Belgium, the Netherlands, and Luxembourg) that established the European Economic Community better known as the Common Market, also reported seeing, one trafficless early Sunday morning, a shepherd driving his flock of several hundred sheep down the Via del Corso—the main street that bisects the city of Rome.

*   *   *

In the afternoons, Liliane goes to an equestrian center called Circolo San Giorgio, on the Via Cassia, located across the Tiber, over the dangerously narrow Ponte Milvio, the oldest bridge in Rome. She rides a young gray nervous thoroughbred mare called Magali. Colonel d'Inzeo, the riding master, stands in the middle of the vast outdoor ring and shouts instructions—instructions in Italian that Liliane does not always understand. From time to time, one of Colonel d'Inzeo's two sons comes to the Circolo San Giorgio to ride. Piero or Raimondo—Liliane never knows which since they look alike in their immaculate military uniforms, both lean and determined. In the ring, the jumps are quickly raised to Grand Prix standards—the highest level of show jumping—to 1.6 meters high and to 2.0 meters wide. Warming up, Piero or Raimondo slowly canters around the ring, then, when all is ready, he collects his horse and gallops toward the three jumps—jumps known as oxers that consist of two rails set far apart. In the first jump the front rail is lower than the back rail—it is the easiest. In the second jump, the back rail is lower than the front rail—it is the most hazardous, because it can cause an optical illusion. In the third jump—the most difficult—the rails are parallel, all of which Piero or Raimondo takes impossibly, effortlessly, almost soundlessly. He does this several times. Afterward, he pats his horse's neck and trots over to his father. They speak briefly, then Raimondo or Piero waves a hand to the other riders in the ring—a salute, a blessing—and leaves. Heroes of the Italian equestrian sport, the brothers are military officers—Piero a colonel in the Italian Army, Raimondo a major in the Carabinieri. At the 1960 Olympics in Rome, Raimondo wins the show-jumping gold medal on a bay called Posillipo and Piero wins the silver on a big white horse called the Rock.

Did Piero notice how she handled her fidgety horse? Did Raimondo think her an excellent rider—a rider who, one day, might win a gold medal at the Olympics?

Rudy's film, *Villa Borghese* (released in English as *It Happened in the Park*) written by Sergio Amidei and directed by Vittorio De Sica with a distinguished cast that includes De Sica, Gérard Philipe, Micheline Presle, Eduardo De Filippo, and Anna Maria Ferrero, and which consists of six vignettes that take place during a single day—beginning in the morning with a nanny and her charges and ending late at night with a prostitute—in historic Villa Borghese Park, was well received and Rudy is pleased and still more generous.

He buys Francine a pair of diamond earrings and Liliane a gold charm bracelet. The charms are beautifully carved and depict five Roman fountains: Fontana delle Api, Fontana del

Nettuno, Fontana dei Quattro Fiumi, Fontana delle Tartarughe, and Fontana del Tritone. The bracelet is heavy and the charms knock against things and Liliane rarely wears it. (A few years later, she will sell the bracelet, keeping one of the charms as a souvenir—the Fontana del Tritone.)

On a visit to Capri with Rudy and Francine, Liliane imagines another life for herself as, walking down the narrow streets filled with the sweet smell of orange trees and jasmine, she catches sight of romantic-looking villas through closed iron gates or over stucco walls topped with bright bougainvillea and bits of broken glass. A life of well-born luxury and elegance like the one she glimpses on the island, led by handsome, well-dressed Italian men and women, who own fast cars and yachts, have titles and aristocratic names—Ruspoli, Torlonia, Pignatelli—and with whom Rudy is slightly acquainted.

"*Ciao, ciao,* Rudy, how are you?" Putting his hand familiarly on Rudy's shoulder, Giovanni Pignatelli stops at their table while they are having a drink before dinner on the *piazzetta.* "*Permesso?*"—May I? he also says and, without waiting for a reply, he pulls up a chair and signals to the waiter.

He smiles at Francine, but Francine does not smile back.

He and Rudy exchange news, gossip, a bit of business. Before he leaves, he nods toward Liliane.

"Your daughter has grown a lot since last summer. A real young lady. *Carina*"—cute, he also says, smiling at her.

After Giovanni Pignatelli has left, Francine leans over and whispers to Liliane, "He just wants to get inside your pants."

Liliane blushes. She has been watching a young waiter as,

confidently, he maneuvers around the crowded tables with a tray full of glasses, bottles, and ice. She has noticed him on earlier occasions as well, and, on one afternoon when she was walking back to the hotel, their paths had crossed.

"*Ciao*," he said, smiling at her.

"*Ciao*," Liliane answered.

A lot of the customers seem to know him by name. "Marcello!" they call out to him. "Marcello."

"*Si, si, subito, signor*"—Yes, yes, right away, sir, Marcello replies good-naturedly, not paying attention to their demands or hurrying to fill their orders.

When Rudy gets ready to pay the bill, he motions to Marcello, who comes over right away. As Marcello makes change, he looks directly at Liliane and softly begins to sing a song popular that summer:

Tu sei per me la più bella del mondo

You are for me the most beautiful in the world

Again, Liliane blushes.

"Italian men are born singers and liars," Rudy says as he leaves Marcello a tip. "It's in their blood. Come, let's go eat. I'm hungry."

At Gemma's, a restaurant popular among the affluent crowd, Dado Ruspoli, the 9th Prince of Cerveteri, the 9th Marquis of Riano, and the 14th Count of Vignanello and an eccentric playboy who walks around Capri with a parrot on his shoulder and whose opium habit is the subject of much gossip, sits at the next table. Turning in his seat, he asks Liliane if she recommends the spaghetti dish she is eating.

"*Bellina*"—pretty, turning back around, he declares to the others at his table about Liliane.

"Careful," Rudy warns her. "Don't go near him."

"Dado is taking lessons from Orson Welles," Francine tells them. "Apparently they are good friends. Lessons in hypnotism."

"Hypnotism?" Rudy repeats, frowning and shaking his head.

"According to the story I heard, they were sitting together in a café," Francine continues, ignoring Rudy, "and Orson Welles, to show off his occult powers, asked Dado what he would like to see happen next, and Dado said that he would like to see the beautiful girl at the next table spill her drink, a Bloody Mary, down the front of her dress and guess what? Right then and there, the girl spilt her Bloody Mary all over the front of her dress."

After dinner, in a nightclub across from the Quisisana Hotel, Rudy and Francine get up to dance. No sooner are they on the dance floor leaving Liliane to sit alone at the table than a young man comes up and asks her to dance.

Liliane is tempted to say no but she says yes.

"Paolo," the young man says, introducing himself as he holds out his arms to her.

"Liliana," Liliane answers—yet another version of her name.

Cha cha, cha cha cha.

Marcello, she thinks.

But Liliane is of two minds. A part of her wants nothing to do with elegant society or with romance. She wants to lead a boy's independent and adventurous life—the kind of carefree life led by the hero in Elsa Morante's coming-of-age novel, *Arturo's Island*.

> *Nonostante la nostra agiatezza, noi vivevamo come selvaggi. Un paio di mesi dopo la mia nascita, mio padre era partito dall'isola per un'assenza di quasi mezz'anno: lasciandomi nelle braccia del nostro primo garzone. . . . Fu il medesimo garzone che m'insegnò a parlare, a leggere e a scrivere. . . . Mio padre non si curò mai di farmi frequentare le scuole: io vivevo sempre in vacanza. . . .*

> *(Although we were fairly well off, we lived like savages. When I was two months old my father left the island . . . he left me in the care of our first boy servant. . . . It was he who taught me to talk, and to read and write. . . . My father never bothered to send me to school; I was always on holiday. . . .)*

Liliane does not want to live like a savage but the freedom of Arturo's life appeals to her. The novel is set on Procida, a smaller, darker, less frequented island than Capri or Ischia in the Bay of Naples, and home to a national prison. There, Arturo's existence is unfettered, full of make-believe, and solitary—a dog, who doubles as a kind of nursemaid, is his only companion—except for when his unreliable, handsome father, whom Arturo worships, makes his occasional visits.

> *Quanto al fornirmi di scarpe, o di vestiti, mio padre se ne ricordava assai di rado. Nell'estate, io non portavo altro indumento che un paio di calzoni. . . . Solo raramente*

*aggiungevo ai calzoni una maglietta di cotone, troppo corta,
tutta strappata e slentata.*

*(Clothes and shoes and things, my father didn't often remem-
ber. In summer I wore nothing but a pair of trousers. . . . Just
occasionally I wore a cotton shirt too, but it was too short,
and hung around me in tatters.)*

Nor does Liliane want to dress in tatters but, as yet, she
does not know how to think about clothes. Her body is strange
to her—she once was pudgy and slightly overweight and now,
all of a sudden and effortlessly, she has lost her "baby fat" and
is thin—skinny, nearly.

Rudy, however, cares what she wears. "Don't you have anything else to put on besides those slacks?"

"Honey, tomorrow, I'll take you to a shop where you can
buy lots of nice things," Francine says quickly, placing a hand on
Liliane's arm. "And I'll bargain them down," she adds, laughing.

"It's about time—how old are you?" Not letting Liliane
answer, Rudy continues, "Time for you to start dressing like . . ."
He hesitates before he says, "like a lady," and reaches for his
cigarettes.

In the shop, the following morning, Francine persuades
Liliane to put away her one-piece bathing suit and buy a bikini.

"What have you got to hide?" Francine tells Liliane. "You
have a perfectly nice body," she adds.

But the revered, handsome father's mysterious and unpredictable ways in *Arturo's Island* are made clear at the end of the novel

and come as a bitter surprise and disillusion to Arturo, his son. The reason, too, Arturo decides to leave the island of Procida, which signals the end of his idyllic innocent childhood. The father is revealed to be homosexual—or, in the language of the novel, a *parodia* (a parody)—and in love with one of the criminals incarcerated in the island's prison.

"Can we go?" Liliane asks her father.

"Go where?" Rudy says.

"To Procida. We can hire a boat. Go for the day."

"Leave Capri?" Rudy asks, frowning. "Why?"

Instead, Liliane hikes up to the top of the cliff known as Tiberio—a steep, hot, forty-minute climb—where Tiberius, the Roman emperor, spent the last ten years of his life in self-imposed exile. From there, she wants to catch a glimpse of Procida—a black volcanic rock in the sea. One day, she promises herself she will go. Standing on the promontory looking out toward the island, Liliane fantasizes a life there for herself. Married to a fisherman—a fisherman who looks like Marcello—she will live in a pastel-colored, stucco house with an arched balcony that overlooks the sea; the garden will be filled with lemon trees and bougainvillea; she will cook and clean and eventually, too, she will write a novel—a novel much like *Arturo's Island*, only she will call it *Liliane's Island*—and despite the fame and fortune the book will bring her, she will continue to shun the corrupt and materialistic outside world, never forsaking the simple life and pleasures of the island of Procida.

A dark cloud momentarily blots out the sun, darkening the sea, and Liliane turns back. Feeling anxious and alone all of a sudden, she hurries past the remains of Tiberius's villa, a pile of roofless, brick rooms, huge arched chambers that might have served as cisterns and storerooms, the imperial bath, loggias, a walkway lined with columns set at the edge of a sheer escarpment encircling a vertical three-hundred-meter drop down to the sea known as the Salto di Tiberio (the Tiberian Leap), where the emperor was said to have thrown people he disliked to their deaths. Tiberius, too, was well-known for his perverse sexual excesses—the one most alluded to was how he trained young boys known as "nipping minnows" to swim alongside of him, biting at his private parts.

On Capri, Rudy, Francine, and Liliane spend most of their days sunbathing and swimming at Gracie Fields's elegant bathing establishment, La Canzone del Mare (The Song of the Sea), on Marina Piccola. The name La Canzone del Mare, according to the British comedienne, was inspired by the passage in the *Odyssey* where Ulysses, sailing past an island—an island that could well have been Capri—begs his sailors to tie him to the ship's mast so that he won't be tempted by the song of the Sirens intended to lure sailors ashore and to their deaths.

A strong swimmer—thanks to lessons learned at Camp Bueno—Liliane swims freestyle. The Tyrrhenian Sea is warm and she swims as far out as she dares, to where the water turns from an aquamarine to green then, quite abruptly, to a colder navy blue.

"I'm starving," Liliane says, as she sits down at the table, joining Rudy and Francine for lunch.

"You're still wet, but the new bathing suit looks good on you," Rudy says, giving her one of his rare compliments.

Liliane spends the month of August on another island. An island in Penobscot Bay, Maine, with Irène and Gaby, and Irène cannot help but notice how Liliane is changed.

"You've lost weight, you look wonderful," she tells her. "And did you have a good time with your father?"

"What did you do?" Irène also asks.

"Nothing much. I went riding every day and we went to Capri," Liliane answers.

"How is Rudy?" Irène says, then hesitating, she asks, "Does he have—someone in his life? A woman, I mean."

Liliane shakes her head. How can she explain to Irène about Francine? "He's busy making movies," she says instead.

Unconvinced, Irène nods.

For several generations, Gaby's family has been spending every summer on this island in Maine. Gaby's grandfather built the house—a large, shingled, three-story gabled house euphemistically referred to as a cottage—situated on a point, a few hundred feet from the water. Jutting out from the shore, below the house, is a granite pier with a float, and several boats—a twenty-foot Herreshoff sailboat, a Boston whaler, and a wooden dinghy. The sailboat, named the *Edwina,* is Gaby's pride and joy and, several times a week, Gaby rows out in the dinghy to bail out the boat, clean the teak, and polish the brass fittings.

"Nathanael Greene Herreshoff was one of the greatest naval architects," Gaby likes to remind Liliane. "Not only did he revolutionize yacht design but he himself sailed five winning America's Cup yachts. . . ." Gaby pauses to recollect their names. "The *Vigilant,* the *Defender,* the *Columbia,* the *Reliance,* and the *Resolute,*" he recites before continuing. "Herreshoff also invented the streamlined bulb and fin keels, the crosscut sail, the modern turnbuckle, the modern winch, sail tracks on masts—"

Either Liliane has stopped listening or she tries to interrupt, "Gaby, I know. You've already told me."

Gaby is an excellent and competitive sailor; silver trophies, won for races by both him and members of his family, line the mantel in the living room of the house.

Liliane, however, avoids sailing with him. As a captain, Gaby is a despot; he curses and shouts at her. During one race, when Liliane was at the tiller while Gaby was putting up the spinnaker, she accidentally jibed and Gaby nearly fell overboard; worse, they came in last.

Irène does not sail with Gaby either. She prefers playing tennis and golf, sports at which she excels.

The other large cottages that dot the coastline on either side of Gaby's house are owned by families not dissimilar from Gaby's—old-moneyed, Protestant, Ivy Leaguers, members of the same private clubs. Many of the cottages are owned by his relatives: sisters, brothers, cousins, cousins by marriage, and those families, likewise, spend their summers on the island each year.

"I haven't missed a single summer—or maybe just one or two because of the war," Gaby says proudly. "I know every last person on the island. Most of them are related to me," he adds.

"The locals, too," Gaby says. "I know them all by name."

The locals on the island live inland in houses that are much smaller. Mostly they work as caretakers, gardeners, cooks, boatmen, and caddies for the summer people. Since the island population is small and, in winter, often cut off from the mainland, many of the local families have intermarried with unfortunate results. Malcolm is one. A caddy, he once unzipped his pants in front of Irène's foursome and peed on the green of the fifth hole.

The island is accessible from the mainland only by ferryboat. It is beautiful with its rocky shore, pine trees, and fields going down to the sea. It is also exclusive, with few stores, no movie theaters, no restaurants or hotels—in other words, no tourist attractions or accommodations. During the day, most of the summer activities occur at the club—tennis, golf, sailing—while at night, they occur in people's homes, where there is a never-ending series of cocktail and dinner parties and where people flirt, have affairs, drink too much, run their cars off the road or their boats aground. None of these peccadilloes are taken very seriously, only anecdotally, stories to recall and tell the following summer.

"Remember last year . . . or was it two years ago?"—all the summers run together—Gaby asks. "When Pete took Mimi over to the mainland in thick fog to pick up her husband and they got lost and had to spend the night in the boat tied up to a lobster pot?"

Right away, when she gets back from Italy, Liliane fits into the summer routine on the island as if she had never left—all but her bikini. The first time she wears it sunbathing on the lawn, Liliane overhears Irène and Gaby as they sit having drinks on the deck directly above her.

"Lillian fills out that little bathing suit quite nicely," Gaby says.

"In Europe, everyone wears bikinis," Irène answers.

"Maybe so, but they don't wear them in Maine."

Liliane can, she thinks, bicycle back and forth in her sleep to the tennis club, the yacht club, the single store that sells newspapers and magazines, scented pine cushions, and ice cream. The same small group of girls her age—Christine, Missy, and Phyllis—are there every summer. Privileged, rich, athletic, they are her good friends. Together, they play tennis, sail, water-ski. If the weather is bad, they stay indoors, bake brownies, and play Monopoly.

There are a few boys.

Not much goes on with the boys—boys whose first names sound like last names: Carlton, Jackson, and Porter. They appear young. Liliane and Christine steal a bunch of golf carts with them one night and ride around the golf course, tracking the greens; on another night they shoot out the streetlamp in front of the post office with a BB gun; on still another night, they go to the local pub—a trailer with a jukebox, part of the floor cleared for dancing—and watch the only couple on it (Fred, the boy who rolls and sweeps out the tennis courts, and an overweight teenage girl, who works as one of the cashiers in the only market on the island, locked in an embrace, hardly moving) and they smoke and drink a few beers.

Liliane is reading *Peyton Place*. The novel has been passed back and forth among her friends so many times that when Liliane finally gets it, the pages containing certain passages are ear-marked and worn—especially worn is the passage that occurs immediately after Allison MacKenzie loses her virginity to the handsome, urbane, married literary agent, Brad Holmes:

> *"It is never as good as it should be for a woman, the first time," he said. "This one will be for you."*
>
> *He began to woo her again, with words, and kisses, and touches, and this time she had felt the full, soaring joy of pleasure without pain.*
>
> *"I thought I was dying," she said to him afterward. "And it was the loveliest feeling in the world."*

"Do you really think it's all that great, Lil?" Phyllis asks Liliane.

Liliane does not know. She has only been as far as second base—and only twice with Porter. Each time, he squeezed and pressed her breasts in such a way that instead of giving her pleasure, he hurt her.

"I doubt my parents ever make love—or maybe they did once and conceived me," Missy says, and the other girls laugh.

"The part that really got to me was the one where Lucas rapes Selena. Can you imagine, your own father?" Christine says.

"Stepfather," Missy corrects her.

IX

The following summer, Xavier Cugat's mambos, sambas, rumbas, and his sultry fourth wife, Abbe Lane, singing "Strangers in the Dark" are the rage in Rome and Liliane takes some of Josephine Baker's beauty advice to heart. She goes out dancing nearly every night. *A cigarette, a spark,* Liliane has started to smoke, to drink a little, *And love walks in,* and she has boyfriends. As yet, she has not slept with any of them.

Mario is short, blond, stocky, and does not look Italian. Enrolled at Sapienza University, he is studying to be a lawyer. Over the bed in Mario's one-room apartment in Trastevere, a mirror hangs from the ceiling. Liliane can look up and watch as she and Mario almost have sex. Afterward, before driving her home—Rudy, either out himself or a heavy sleeper, does not hear her come in—Mario stops at a café in a working-class district of the city where the other customers are just starting out their day. They watch as Mario and Liliane order a glass of red wine—clearly the two have been making love all night and are thirsty—and, among themselves, the other customers wink and make suggestive remarks. In spite of feeling like an impostor, Liliane is pleased to be the center of their attention.

Paul is twenty-seven, much older than Liliane. On meeting him one afternoon at the Café de Paris on the Via Veneto, immediately, and for no reason except that he is darkly handsome, slender, and elegant, Liliane falls in love with him. Paul is Moroccan, from Casablanca—which he refers to familiarly as "Casa." His family is in the sugar business—no doubt, Cosumar, the company founded in 1929 that specializes in the production of sugar loafs, sugar ingots, sugar lumps, and granulated sugar refined from local sugar beets. Paul and his family are friends of Sultan Mohammed V, the king of Morocco. Paul does not need to work. Restless, he dates beautiful models and famous movie stars, one of whom is Silvana Mangano.

Liliane is young and pretty and Paul teases and flirts with her. He takes her to *Belvedere delle Rose,* the same nightclub where a few years earlier Liliane had heard Claudia sing *fado* and where the stripper had turned out to be a man. Along with the band, a woman croons in English:

Dance me to the moon

On the dance floor, Liliane feels as if everyone in the nightclub is looking at them—the women especially, who no doubt are wondering how Liliane deserves to have Paul's smooth dark cheek pressed against hers—but Liliane does not care.

Paul is a good dancer, easy to follow, and Liliane has never been happier than in his arms. *Can this be love? Or the magic of?*

When Paul is called back to "Casa" on family business, Liliane accompanies him to the airport. On the way, in the taxi, Paul hands Liliane a pair of white kid gloves, saying how the night before a woman had left them in his hotel room and could Liliane, please, return them to her. Liliane says she will and Paul writes down the woman's address. But after Paul has gone and Liliane is on her way back to the city, she starts to cry.

"*Signorina*," the taxi driver says, looking at her in his rearview mirror and shaking his head, "*non preoccuparti, io sono sicuro che tornerà a voi*"—Miss, don't worry, I am sure he will come back to you.

Not answering the taxi driver and still crying, Liliane throws the white kid gloves out the taxi window.

To you
My heart cries out "Perfidia"
For I find you, the love of my life
In somebody else's arms

Sergio too, is older. He was married—married for four months and the marriage was annulled. Ivy, his former wife, is a model but the trouble with Ivy, Sergio tells Liliane, is that she can only talk about shoes and about clothes, but he still sees her from time to time. Handsome—not as handsome as Paul—in a brooding sort of way, Sergio designs light fixtures and furniture and as it turns out—Liliane will find this out only much later—prefers boys to girls.

Liliane does not remember how Sergio said he met Alberto Moravia and his wife, Elsa Morante, but he talks about them a great deal. He describes to Liliane how beautiful and talented Elsa is and how generous she can be—every night inviting six or eight people, most of them young men, for dinner and afterward paying the bill. Also, Sergio describes her rooftop terrace filled with bougainvillea and flowering fruit trees, and the view of Piazza del Popolo below.

"I'd like to meet her." Liliane has told Sergio several times. "I loved *Arturo's Island*," she adds.

"I will arrange it," Sergio promises her.

Instead, Sergio drives Liliane in his brand-new blue two-seat Fiat 500—designed by Dante Giacosa and known as the Cinquecento, which Sergio tells Liliane cost him 490,000 lire—to Fregene to have lunch with Alberto Moravia. Moravia's house, Sergio also tells her, is on the beach and they can go swimming.

"Did you bring your bathing suit?" Sergio asks. "I forgot mine. Anyway, it's hazy and overcast, not a nice day," he says.

"I don't want to go in the ocean by myself," Liliane says. "There might be an undertow."

On account of the traffic that day, Sergio and Liliane are late. Already, Moravia and a tall, elegantly dressed woman who is not Elsa Morante and whose name is Claire—she appears to be English—are standing by the front door, waiting for them.

"Hurry up if you want to go swimming," Moravia says to them. "We will wait lunch for you."

"No, no, I don't want to go swimming," Sergio says, then pointing to Liliane, adds, "but she does."

The water is choppy and gray and Liliane can feel Moravia, Claire, and Sergio watching her as, determined to show them that she is unafraid, she adjusts the straps to her bathing suit and runs into the sea. If she drowns, she thinks, it will be Sergio's fault.

When Liliane comes back from swimming, everyone—Moravia, Claire, and Sergio—is already sitting at the table eating lunch, not waiting for her.

"Sit. Sit down here," Moravia tells her, motioning to the empty chair next to him.

"I have to change," Liliane says. "I'm in my wet bathing suit."

Getting up from the table, the Englishwoman, Claire, takes Liliane into a bedroom—Alberto Moravia's bedroom.

On the dresser is a framed photograph of Alberto Moravia and Elsa Morante. They are on a beach, another beach, and Moravia is sitting with one leg bent—perhaps, his bad leg; he had coxitis as a child—and Elsa, wearing a two-piece bathing suit, is standing next to him. Neither one is looking at the other.

Opening the door to the bedroom without knocking, Moravia asks, "Are you coming or not?" His tone is abrupt, almost angry.

"Ah, Elsa," he says, relenting a little as he sees Liliane quickly put down the photograph.

"That was taken when we were living in Capri. We were just married and poor and Capri was cheap and beautiful . . ." Moravia's voice trails off, then he says, "But come, let's have lunch."

During lunch, Moravia continues, "We rented an apartment in Anacapri—the apartment belonged to the mayor—and we had a beautiful view of the Bay of Naples from our balcony. We worked all morning—I on my novel *Agostino* and Elsa on *Menzogna e Sortilegio*—in English, *House of Liars*," Moravia translates

for Liliane's benefit. "Afterward we walked down to Capri, then to the beach. We went everywhere on foot because we had no money and later we had to walk all the way back up again. Often we quarreled the whole way." Moravia shakes his head at the recollection.

"Elsa had her Siamese cat on a leash and I had an owl on my shoulder. The people in the village must have thought us very eccentric but they were kind, hospitable, and honest. We never locked our doors. The war was going on but we knew almost nothing. We did not have a radio and the newspapers, when there were any, were old and out-of-date. Occasionally, Elsa and I walked up to look at the cannons that were supposed to defend the Bay of Naples but they appeared old and rusty and I doubt if they could have fired a single shot. Mostly, we led a simple and productive life in Capri."

"What was Elsa like then?" Liliane summons up the courage to ask Moravia.

"She was quarrelsome and stubborn," Moravia replies, drinking some wine. "For instance, she did not know how to swim and nothing I said could persuade her to learn. She claimed she was too old. She was twenty-eight.

"How old are you?" Moravia suddenly asks Liliane. "Seventeen, eighteen?"

Without waiting for her reply, Moravia continues, "Elsa was also brave. In the fall of 1943, we were living in our small attic flat on Via Sgambati—we had left Capri by then although, in retrospect, we should have stayed—and Mussolini had just been arrested and the Fascists in their blackshirts were marching all over Rome waving banners that said *Viva la morte!*—Long live death! Again Moravia interrupts himself to tell Liliane, "You are too young to remember any of this. But it was then," he continues, "that I learned that I was on their wanted list and was going to be arrested. Elsa and I packed a suitcase and we took the first train to Naples. I still remember what I was wearing—a double-breasted linen suit, and Elsa was wearing a light cotton dress." Moravia pauses a moment to smile and shake his head. "It was September and the weather was warm and we assumed that the British would arrive in the next few days and liberate the city of Naples. The train, however, did not go to Naples. All of a sudden it stopped in a deserted-looking station and we were told to get off. The conductor said there were no more train tracks. It was a beautiful day, the countryside was filled with the sound of cicadas and Elsa and I set off."

Sergio, Claire, and Liliane have hardly said a word. Only the servant clearing the antipasto plates and bringing clean ones for the pasta, speaks. "*Caldo. Fate attenzione*"—Hot. Be careful, he says about the plates.

"We lived for nine months in a one-room hut built against the side of a rock in a village called Sant'Agata, in the mountainous region of Ciociara," Moravia continues after helping himself to spaghetti and to the sauce. "The bed was made out of a plank with a sack of corn for a mattress; the floor of the hut was packed earth and when it rained, we stood ankle-deep in water. There were no pens or paper; the only books we had brought along were the Bible and *The Brothers Karamazov*—we used the pages of the latter for toilet paper. We got water from the well to wash and we shared one meal a day with the peasants—bread, beans, a glass of acidic local wine.

"We did absolutely nothing during those nine months. We stared at the rocky landscape and waited for the Allies to arrive. From time to time, we could hear bombs dropping in the town of Fondi or we looked up at the sky and watched dogfights between the German and the British. Twice Elsa and I were strafed by planes as we were walking. Once by an English Spitfire, the other by a squadron of American Flying Fortresses. Each time we managed to save ourselves by lying down in a nearby ditch."

Moravia stops talking for a moment to eat his pasta. He expertly wraps the spaghetti around his fork pressed against his spoon and eats quickly, noisily.

"But you asked me about Elsa," he says to Liliane.

"I was the one who was wanted by the Fascists, but Elsa chose to stay with me. She endured all the discomforts and miseries and never complained. Also, she did a very courageous thing. In October, when it began to get cold—I told you that we had brought only one suitcase with nothing but summer things—Elsa went back to Rome by herself to get some warm clothes. She went to our apartment on Via Sgambati and packed another suitcase—ironically, a German soldier helped her carry the heavy suitcase at the train station—and she returned to Sant'Agata. Elsa also had a chance to stop and check on her manuscript of *Menzogna e Sortilegio*, which she had left behind with a friend. It was safe. That was all she cared about—that and me," Moravia adds with a slight grimace.

"In 1943, Edwin, my brother, parachuted into Sicily with the 1st Airborne—" Claire starts to say but Moravia cuts her off.

"Yes, yes, you've told us already."

Then turning to Liliane, he asks, "Have you been?"

"To Sicily?"

"No. Capri."

"Oh, Capri. Yes, I went there last summer with my father and his lady friend," Liliane answers. "It's a beautiful island," she adds.

Again, Moravia has lost interest and does not comment. Instead, he calls for the waiter who comes in hurriedly and begins to clear the plates.

"We have cheese and fruit for dessert," Moravia announces. "Local cheese and pears from Emilia-Romagna."

After lunch, Moravia tells Sergio that he will drive Liliane home and Sergio is to take Claire back to Rome.

Sergio says nothing, Claire tells Sergio that she knows Ivy, his former wife, and Liliane tries to protest.

"But I came with Sergio and I should go back—" she starts to say.

"Where do you live?" Moravia interrupts her.

When Liliane tells him, Moravia says, "That's on my way."

On account of Moravia's bad leg, his car is singular, custom-built—something to do with the clutch he depresses to change gears. The way Moravia drives, too, is singular—fast, with one hand on Liliane's thigh.

The whole time in the car on the way back to Rome from Fregene, Liliane thinks how the next time she sees Sergio she will not mince words. She will tell him how Moravia drove at a hundred miles an hour with his hand on her leg and that she doesn't care how famous Moravia is or that, afterward, she can tell people she has met him—she could have been killed.

As it turns out, however, driving back in the brand-new Fiat 500 designed by Dante Giacosa, Sergio is the one who has an accident. He gets a blowout and loses control of the car; the car goes through the highway guardrail and down off an embankment. Fortunately, Sergio is not hurt but Claire, sitting next to him in the front seat, is killed.

The next summer, instead of going to Rome or to the island in Penobscot Bay, Liliane stays in New York by herself—Irène has gone up to Maine and Gaby comes down to the city only for a few days in July. She has a job working at a travel agency in midtown; the travel agency is located in the basement of a hotel and has no windows. Liliane's job is to type and to file. Filing is okay and boring but typing is more of a challenge. Usually, Liliane waits until all the other office workers have left for the day before she distributes all her bungled typed sheets of paper into different wastebaskets.

After work, Liliane meets up with her friend Moira in the Horn & Hardart Automat on West Fifty-seventh Street. They buy a cup of coffee before they go to Ballet Arts located in Carnegie Hall. Never mind that Liliane has taken up dancing late, she is passionate about ballet. For a while, she thinks of nothing else—of her extension, of her pliés, of being thin. Moira, her best friend, is equally obsessed and they take classes together. Moira, however, wants to be an actor. Already, she has auditioned for several Broadway roles, including the part of Anne in *The Diary of Anne Frank.*

"If only Lee Strasberg was my father," Moira says about Susan Strasberg getting the part of Anne Frank.

"I read how Strasberg said he was amazed by Susan's performance," Liliane says. "He said he had no idea where she picked up acting, she has never had any formal training."

"Right." Moira rolls her eyes.

Carrying their tote bags full of slippers, leotards, tights, leg warmers, Liliane and Moira go to their class.

Vladimir Dokoudovsky was born in 1919 of Russian parents and was a principal dancer with Colonel W. de Basil's Ballet Russe de Monte Carlo, where his roles included the Polovtsian Dances from *Prince Igor*, the Golden Slave in *Scheherazade*, and the nimble Harlequin in *Carnaval*. He also danced the title roles of *Pétrouchka* and *Paganini*. Forced to retire from performing on account of severe arthritis, he began to teach at Ballet Arts Studio 61 in 1947.

A highly demanding and commanding presence, Dokoudovsky is nicknamed the Duke by his students. Standing in the middle of the room, dressed in black pants, a white billowing shirt, and a red silk sash wrapped tightly around his slim waist, he carries a stick with which he beats out the time.

At the barre, Liliane and Moira stand straight and nervous. Dokoudovsky commands, "Dégagé in fifth":

Right leg—dégagé front, side, back
Left leg—dégagé front
Right—dégagé front, side, back
Left—dégagé back
Right—dégagé front
Left—passé back to front
Left—passé front to back
Right—dégagé front
Left—dégagé back
Right—passé front to back
Right—passé back to front
Left—dégagé back
Right—dégagé front
Left—dégagé back
Right—dégagé front
Left—dégagé back

"Turn. Repeat," Dokoudovsky orders. Then he says, "You"— he walks over to an Asian girl at the barre in front of Liliane and brandishes his stick as if to strike her with it—"you are not paying attention. If you cannot pay attention, please leave my class."

During the entire summer of classes, neither Liliane nor Moira speak to Dokoudovsky; nor does he speak to them.

Across the hall, Nina Stroganova, Dokoudovsky's former wife and a ballerina in her own right, holds another class. Originally

Danish, she is petite and blonde and, to teach, she wears an assortment of colorful clothes as well as strapped high-heel shoes. She
calls her students by their first names and is encouraging.

Liliane and Moira prefer Dokoudovsky's class.

"He is more challenging," Moira says.

"He's handsome in a tormented sort of way. Like Heathcliff," Liliane adds.

"Ha," Moira gives a knowing laugh.

Liliane has begun writing a novel. The novel is about her imagined life with Heathcliff during the three years he spent away from Wuthering Heights—no mention is ever made by Emily Brontë where Heathcliff went or how he made his fortune during that time. Liliane calls her novel *The Manor*. The novel begins by describing it:

The manor is a chain of low gray buildings of different sizes with four square turrets that form the corners and tower above them. There is a large courtyard in the center and, to the left, the kennels and stables. The manor was built during the reign of Queen Elizabeth and although it has since been enlarged, the central part and the kitchen have not changed. The drive to the manor is several miles long and begins outside the village of S., which is named after the manor. The road itself has not been kept up as it should, but in places the view is breathtaking, especially after a small and final rise when the manor house suddenly appears, stretched out immense, below. More vivid still, is the countryside, for its intense sense of desolation and wildness. Here, the green, well-cut lawns, carefully trimmed alleys and rolling hills do not exist. Instead there are perilous bogs and marshes. The trees are sparse and bent and the underbrush so thick and thorny that it tears through thick woolen stockings into the flesh. The farmland is meager and hard to cultivate. This is the pays sans nom—country without a name—where Heathcliff and I live.

The novel goes on to describe a season when Heathcliff and the narrator entertain and their house is filled with guests:

All the candles are lit and the rooms are heated with great fires in which gigantic logs crackle and burn. In the darkly polished dining hall, the silver tableware catches the reflection of the candelabras and gleams almost blindingly as Heathcliff gets up to carve the roast, flashing the carving knife like a Roman gladiator his sword. . . .

(Long afterward, Moira will remind Liliane of this awful simile.)

Set during yet another season when Heathcliff and Liliane alone inhabit the manor house, the last paragraph of Liliane's unfinished novel goes like this:

Upstairs in the bedroom, it is colder and the moan of the wind is more penetrating. The room rocks with the sound. Swiftly, we get undressed, the floor cold under our bare feet, and climb into bed under the heavy quilts and Heathcliff, with one easy motion, blows out the only candle.

On the weekends, Liliane goes farther afield—downtown, to lower Fifth Avenue, to Erick Hawkins's studio.

A tall, craggy-faced man, Erick Hawkins begins his class by telling his students to lie down on the floor and roll.

"Roll, roll, roll. But don't roll into anyone. Preserve your own space," he says.

"Keep rolling. Don't be afraid," Erick Hawkins says again.

In Aaron Copland's *Appalachian Spring*, Martha Graham, wrapped in her long red dress, rolled back and forth onstage. The ballet premiered in 1944 and Erick Hawkins had danced the part of the husbandman with her. He had joined Martha Graham's company in 1939 as the first male dancer; then he and Martha married in 1948; a few years later, in 1954, they divorced—due to conflicting artistic egos.

Rejecting the rigidity of ballet as well as the belief held by Martha Graham that dance movement is the expression of inner emotion, Hawkins's works celebrate the human body and nature. He believed in what he called "suchness"—a central concept in Zen Buddhism expressing the true essence of reality—and sought to achieve in dance, in his own words, "just the pure poetry of movement."

Back on her feet after rolling on the floor for several minutes, Liliane stands at the barre. Barefoot and bare-legged, she lifts her leg high in her hip socket.

Standing in the center of the room and showing them how, Erick Hawkins tells his students, "Initiate the movement from your pelvic center." He wears loose, pajama-like white cotton pants and is bare-chested; he, too, is barefoot.

"I want you to achieve a sense of lightness, of freedom," he continues.

"Find the body's midline," he also says.

Walking over to Liliane, he puts his hands on her hips and tries to correct her stance.

"You are too tight," he says. "Tight muscles cannot feel. Only effortless, free-flowing muscles are sensuous," he adds.

Still holding her by a hip with one hand, Erick Hawkins

takes Liliane's leg with his other hand and lifting it higher, he swings the leg back and forth.

"Think of yourselves as a door," he tells Liliane. "A beautiful door opening, a beautiful door closing."

Liliane and Moira eat little. Liliane weighs 108 pounds; shorter, Moira weighs less. If they do eat—if, for instance, Moira comes over to Liliane's apartment and they cook a batch of brownies and eat them all—they stick their fingers down their throats and make themselves throw up. They regularly take Benzedrine and laxatives; in addition, they smoke. Liliane is proud of the way her hips stick out—like knives, she says. Pinching at her midriff, Moira claims not to have a single ounce of body fat.

Once a week, Irène telephones Liliane from the house in Maine.

"How are you, *chérie*?" she asks.

"Is everything all right? You are not too lonely in the apartment by yourself?"

Without waiting for an answer, Irène continues, "Are any of your friends in the city?"

"Moira is here," Liliane says.

"The actress?" Irène asks.

Since Liliane does not answer, Irène says, "And your job? Not too boring, I hope."

"No, it's okay. And anyway, I have ballet."

"You're taking ballet? You didn't tell me."

"Moira and I take a few classes after work," Liliane says.

"At night? Isn't that dangerous? And are you eating? I told you, didn't I, that you could charge food at the Gristedes down the street?"

"Yes, I know. I do," Liliane lies.

"I don't want you to starve," Irène says with a laugh.

"Don't worry. I'm fine."

"Oh, and I nearly forgot to tell you—Gaby is coming down to the city next week for a few days. He has business, but he wants to take you out to dinner one night."

"Fine," Liliane says again.

"And, if you have dinner with Gaby, please don't talk to him about politics," Irène adds. "You know how he hates Adlai Stevenson and how angry he gets if you mention his name."

Liliane starts to say something about how Adlai Stevenson is in favor of limiting all hydrogen bomb test detonations aboveground but Irène cuts her off.

"Promise me," she says, "you won't argue with him."

"Then it's okay if we all die from nuclear fallout," Liliane says, determined to have the last word.

The first day Gaby is back in the city, Liliane does not see him. In the morning, she is off to work before Gaby is up—or so she assumes, as the door to his and Irène's bedroom is shut. In the evening, when she comes back from ballet class, Gaby is not home yet. The only evidence she has that he has been in the apartment is a dirty glass—the glass smells of bourbon—in the kitchen sink.

On the second day, Liliane has just gotten into bed and turned out the light when she hears her bedroom door open.

"Lillian, are you awake?" Gaby says.

Didn't anyone teach you to knock? Liliane thinks.

She hesitates, not sure whether to answer him.

"Good night, Lillian," he says.

She is silent.

But instead of shutting the door and leaving, Gaby steps into her room. His step, Liliane can tell, is unsteady. He reaches for the wall for balance, then for a chair to steady himself.

"Lillian," he says again, his voice slurred, "are you asleep?"

Better not to answer him, Liliane decides: Gaby sounds drunk.

In the dark, Gaby trips over something lying on the floor—her shoes, Liliane guesses—and catches himself by grabbing at the foot of Liliane's bed.

"Damn," he mutters.

Lying on her back, Liliane does not move.

Go away. Please, go away, she says to herself.

Gaby comes alongside her bed; with his hand he gropes until he finds her—his hand slides up her legs, her hips her stomach, until they reach her breasts.

Liliane shuts her eyes; she hardly dares breathe.

Go, go, go, she says again to herself. *Please, God, make him go.*

"Darling," Gaby mumbles as, grunting, he climbs up on Liliane's bed and lies on top of her. He lies there without moving, his body heavy. His cheek, rough with stubble, pressed against hers, his breath smells of bourbon.

Only a single cotton sheet separates them and, although her heart is pounding, Liliane wills herself not to move. Inexplicably, a song she has not thought of or sung in years starts up inside her head:

Il etait un petit navire,
Qui n'avait ja-ja jamais navigué,
Ohé! Ohé! Ohé! Ohé! Matelot, . . .
Matelot navigue sur les flots

There was once a little boat,
That had never sailed,
Ahoy! Ahoy!
Ahoy! Ahoy! Sailor,
Sailor on the high seas

After a few minutes, Gaby begins to snore. One of his snores wakes him, and slowly, awkwardly, muttering something Liliane does not catch, Gaby heaves himself up and leaves Liliane's room.

Ohé! Ohé!
Ohé! Ohé! Matelot.

In the morning, shaved and dressed, Gaby is in the kitchen. He is making coffee.

"Do you want a cup?" he asks Liliane.

Shaking her head, Liliane does not look at him.

"You must have been out late last night," Gaby continues in an ordinary voice. "I didn't hear you come in."

"No . . . yes," Liliane does not know what to answer him or what he is talking about.

"How's work?" Gaby asks in a friendly voice.

"It's okay," Liliane answers.

"I've got to go," she also says.

"See you, Lillian," Gaby calls out after her.

That night, again, Gaby comes into her room and lies on top of her.

The next day, Irène telephones and asks, "How are you, *chérie?*"

Then she says, "Let me speak to Gaby. Is he there?"

"He's not here." Liliane has trouble controlling her voice.

"*Chérie,*" Irène says again, alarmed. "Is anything the matter?"

In spite of herself, Liliane lets out a sob, which she turns into a cough.

"Are you sick?"

"No, everything is fine," she manages to answer.

"But have you seen Gaby?" Irène persists.

"No," Liliane tells Irène, "I haven't seen him."

X

A year earlier, during Liliane's senior year in high school, Irène overdoses on sleeping pills. In the morning, a Sunday, unable to wake her, Gaby called the family doctor—Dr. Fischer's successor—at home.

"Get her up and walk her," the doctor told Gaby. "The important thing is to keep her moving."

"I'll call an ambulance," he also said.

Gaby and Liliane lifted Irène out of bed; then, holding her up by the arms, they stood her up. Irène's eyes were closed and her blonde hair was matted; her feet barely touch the floor. Her pink silk nightgown was bunched up around her waist and Liliane tried to cover Irène with her wrapper, but it slipped to the floor.

"Never mind that now, Lillian," Gaby told her. "Let's go."

Together, they walk Irène up and down the apartment hall until the paramedics arrived with a stretcher.

"Is she going to be all right?" Liliane asked one of them.

Already, Irène showed signs of life by moaning and shaking her head.

"No," she said twice, as the paramedics strapped her onto the stretcher.

"I'll call you," Gaby said to Liliane as he followed the paramedics carrying Irène on the stretcher out the door.

Gaby forgot to call Liliane and only later when he returned to the apartment did he say something vague to her about Irène's fragile nerves breaking and for Liliane not to worry. Irène would be home in a couple of days.

"Right as rain," Gaby said.

"I'm beat," he also said. "I feel as if I haven't slept in a week. I'm going to bed. Good night, Lillian," he added.

Brigid, the cleaning lady, was no more informative. "The lady I used to work for—God love her," Brigid told Liliane, "a beautiful lady like your mother, and she had a nice apartment, a husband, two children, and you'd think, wouldn't you, with all of that, that she would be happy—" Brigid stopped and crossed herself, saying, "Sweet Mary, Mother of God."

"What happened to her?" Liliane asked Brigid.

Instead of answering, Brigid crossed herself again. "Nerves is what they called it. But will you look at me," she said, "standing around talking as if I had all day and I've got the sheets still to iron and all of the mister's shirts."

"In the Middle Ages, a nervous breakdown was called melancholia," Liliane read in a medical dictionary in her school library, while, earlier, according to Hippocrates, melancholia was caused by an excess of black bile, hence the name in Ancient

Greek—μέλας (melas)—meaning "black." But Irène was much too fair and too beautiful to be filled with an ugly substance that, Liliane imagined, looked like the black viscous oil that goes into the engine of a car.

Although melancholics suffered, they were thought to be more creative, and Liliane thought of Irène's paintings—in particular, the one of a woman dressed entirely in green sitting alone in an orange room that was a kind of anti-portrait of Irène.

"Green," Irène had said, "is my least favorite color. It soaks up the light."

"Will you go to the studio?" Liliane asks her mother once Irène is home again. Liliane was back early from school; she no longer stopped off at her friend Pamela's apartment to smoke cigarettes and drink Coke laced with rum. She was afraid for Irène, at the same time that she felt vaguely responsible for her. Although midafternoon and outside the sun was shining, the curtains were drawn in the living room. Not yet dressed, Irène was in her bathrobe.

Shaking her head, Irène said, "No, I don't think so."

"Why? You enjoyed it and your paintings are lovely," Liliane said.

"Please," Irène said, looking all of a sudden as if she might cry.

Liliane was silent.

The medical dictionary had gone on to describe how in the tradition of melancholy, a person feels an inexplicable sense of loss and Liliane could not help but count up Irène's: the loss of the sunny apartment in the Charlottenburg district of Berlin; the loss of her parents—despite her fraught relationship with Waldemar and the absent, ineffectual Louise—the loss of her home on Rue Raynouard in Paris and all her belongings, including the silver, the china, the paintings, and her elegant Patou suits and her Revillon furs; the loss of Rudy, even though Irène has admitted that she was never in love with him.

"I respected your father," she had told Liliane, "but I was always a bit afraid of him."

"Why did you marry him then?"

"I had to get away. Get away from my parents, get away from Germany."

"But you must have had other reasons," Liliane persisted.

"Rudy was kind." Irène stopped a moment to reflect. "He was generous," she added.

"But still . . ." Liliane said.

"I was very young and ignorant. I had never had a boyfriend," Irène tried to justify herself. "As a matter of fact," Irène continued after a lengthy pause during which she repeatedly smoothed the lap of her robe, "I was frightened. Even after we were married, I wouldn't sleep with your father."

"What?"

"It's true," Irène confessed, "and he never forced me. He said he would wait until I was ready."

Again, Liliane is silent.

"Tonight?" Rudy asks Irène each night before he goes to bed.

"No, not tonight," Irène answers.

"Soon?"

"Yes, soon, I promise you."

"You know I love you."

"I know."

"You know I would never hurt you."

Irène does not answer.

"Good night, darling," Rudy says after waiting a moment longer, then he leaves the bedroom and goes into the next room to try to sleep.

"Good night," Irène answers.

"And when were you . . . ready, I mean?" Liliane had asked her mother.

Embarrassed, Irène shrugged. "Silly of me, I shouldn't have told you that. And, of course, I had you, *chérie.* That should answer your question."

The loss of Claude.

Claude, the love of Irène's life—romantic, dashing, impetuous, charming, lucky, sexy Claude!

Rudy, on the other hand, was in love with Irène.

"How is your mother?" Is the first thing Rudy always asks Liliane when she arrives in Rome.

"Fine," Liliane always answers—not quite true since Irène overdosed she seems quite fragile and nervous. To calm her, the doctor has prescribed Miltown.

"Is she still painting?" Rudy asks.

"Yes, she goes to a studio several times a week."

"I always told her she had talent," Rudy says, sounding pleased. "And what about tennis? She played a good game."

"She won the women's singles championship last summer."

"And Gaby," Rudy asks after a while. "Is he well?"

"He's fine," Liliane answers, although again it is not the truth. Gaby has had a heart attack and was hospitalized for a week. In addition, he has been told to stop smoking and drinking. But Liliane does not tell Rudy this.

* * *

Irène's sister, Barbara, has always liked Rudy.

"We've stayed in touch," she tells Liliane. "Ever since the old Berlin days when we played field hockey at the same club," she gives a laugh, "and even after he and Irène were divorced. And I remember running into him in Paris—it was years ago and the first time I had left Germany since the war—I was attending a conference and all of a sudden there was Rudy walking down the Champs-Élysées. He was with Tolia—do you remember Tolia?" Barbara asks. Not waiting for a reply, she says, "I hadn't seen Tolia in nearly twenty years and the next thing I knew, your father and Tolia were taking me to lunch at an elegant Russian restaurant called Korniloff. We had caviar, a big bowl filled with it—beluga, the best kind, Rudy said—I had never tasted caviar before and Tolia knew all the waiters by name and spoke to them in Russian. We had such a good time talking over old times. Also, I will always be grateful to Rudy." Barbara adds, "I told him how I wanted to go to America but I did not have enough money and right away, he promised to lend me the money. He was so generous."

"Yes," Liliane agrees. "Generous to a fault."

"How is Rudy?" Barbara then asks.

Already nearsighted, Rudy has cataracts in both his eyes.

"He can hardly see," Liliane says. "Yet he insists on driving the Lancia. One day he is bound to have an accident or kill someone."

Somewhere Liliane had read that cataract surgery is one of the oldest medical procedures in history. Bronze instruments that could have been used for that purpose have been found in excavations in Babylonia, Greece, and Egypt. The article went on to describe how the first recorded operation was performed in India in 800 BC by a doctor named Sushruta Samhita, who wrote how he used a curved needle to push the opaque phlegmatic matter out of the way, then how the patient blew it out through his nose, and afterward, how the eye was irrigated in breast milk—disgusted, Liliane did not read further.

In addition, Rudy suffers from severe bouts of gout, caused by elevated levels of uric acid in the blood. The uric acid crystallizes and forms deposits in the joints and tendons causing almost intolerable pain. Rudy is allergic to the medications that act as inhibitors and, each time he has an attack, he has to seek relief with an injection of steroids in the joint that is affected and that, too, is excruciating.

Rudy's health has deteriorated rapidly; he has been in and out of a clinic in Rome. He walks with a cane and his hands— the fingers swollen and curled—are often so stiff that he cannot undo the zipper of his trousers fast enough and, helpless, he pees inside them. "He is having trouble taking proper care of himself," the Italian doctor has warned Liliane. "Too many of his joint surfaces have been destroyed."

"The last time I saw him," Liliane tells Barbara, "he was so lame, he could hardly get across the street." She pauses and shakes her head. "I can't believe how he has changed."

"Poor old Rudy, and he isn't even that old," Barbara says.

"And Tolia," Barbara says, "I wonder what has happened to him. I remember he was in love with Uli. He wanted to marry her. But I always quite liked Tolia," she adds, laughing.

And did you see Tolia again? Liliane wants to ask Barbara but does not.

After lunch at Korniloff, the elegant Russian restaurant, Barbara tells Rudy and Tolia that she has to get back to her conference. Already, she says, she is late. Rudy, too, says he is late for a meeting and he kisses Barbara good-bye.

"Keep in touch," he tells her, "and don't forget my promise."

"I won't forget," Barbara answers. "Thank you."

"Do svidaniya"—good-bye, Rudy tells Tolia.

Turning to Tolia, Barbara starts to say good-bye to him as well.

"Do you really have to go?" Tolia is holding Barbara by the arm. "Can't you stay a bit longer?" he pleads. "We haven't seen each other in such a long time."

She hesitates.

"Come on, Babutz," Tolia says, calling her by her old childhood nickname. "Let's have one more drink—for old time's sake."

Back inside the Russian restaurant, they sit at the bar and order two glasses of vodka—Tolia pronounces it "wodka"—and again two more; then, slightly tipsy, they walk arm in arm the few blocks to Tolia's apartment where they make love.

Afterward, Tolia tells Barbara, "I should have married you, Babutz."

"But Uli was smart to refuse you" is how Barbara, pleased, answers him.

Barbara has stayed in touch with Uli. In her letters, Uli has expressed her concern that the violence occurring in neighboring Kenya will spread to Tanganyika. The group responsible were the Mau Mau, who were made up primarily of members of the Kikuyu tribe seeking land reform and, more important, the end of the British colonial rule. The origin of the name Mau Mau

is unclear and possible explanations are: an anagram for *Uma uma*, which means "get out get out," the range of mountains bordering the Rift Valley, or the Kikuyus' war cry.

The first European Mau Mau casualty occurred in October 1952. Eric Bowyer, who lived on an isolated farm, was surprised by a Mau Mau in his bath where he was hacked to death. His two house servants were also hacked to death. A few months later, on January 1, 1953, Charles Ferguson and Richard Bingley, who were dining together in Ferguson's remote farmhouse in the Thomson Falls district, were hacked to death and dismembered. Twenty-three days later, another attack became the most notorious and most sensationalized Mau Mau crime. Roger Ruck, a farmer in the Rift Valley, and his pregnant wife, Esmee, a doctor who ran a dispensary for Africans, were taking an evening stroll in their garden before going to bed when thirty Mau Mau attacked them with their machetes. The Rucks were slashed to death and their bodies were left on the veranda. The attackers then ransacked and looted their house. Upstairs, they found six-year-old Michael Ruck asleep in his bed and they killed him as well. (Newspapers both abroad and in Kenya, published gruesome photos of Michael and his bloodstained toys lying scattered all over his bedroom floor.)

These last three killings, which were reported in the British papers, sent the white community into a panic. What made things worse was the rumor that the Mau Mau had been let into the Rucks' house by the cook. The servants' collusion in the murders of their masters made the attacks more frightening and unpredictable and made every black man suspect.

Graham Greene, a journalist in Kenya at the time and a contrarian, tried to make light of the situation and wrote: "To the English, it was like a revolt of the domestic staff. It was as though Jeeves had taken to the jungle and had sworn, however unwillingly, to kill Bertie Wooster." A year later, the burning down of the fashionable Treetops Hotel, where Princess Elizabeth was staying with Prince Philip when she learned of King George VI's death and her succession to the throne of Great Britain, by Mau Mau activists was another blow to British authority.

The Mau Mau's savage attacks were not restricted to the white population. They also attacked their own—Kikuyus who were loyal to the British. The most brutal instance took place on the night of March 25, 1953, in the settlement of Lari, where the Mau Mau herded the villagers into their huts then threw gasoline on the thatch roofs, setting them on fire and burning alive the people trapped inside; they also viciously hacked down anyone who tried to escape, throwing them back into the flaming huts, thus killing ninety-seven innocent Kikuyu men, women, and children.

The British were no less brutal. Once a state of emergency was declared, they launched mass arrests and deportations. First screening centers, then detention camps—more like concentration camps—were set up and designed as a rehabilitation program, known as the *Pipeline*. Their goal was to interrogate and make the detainees renounce their Mau Mau oath. Conditions were harsh—little food, no sanitation, enforced silence—and brutality, torture, and mutilation were the standard procedures for the treatment of the detainees; a huge number of men were hung without even a semblance of a trial. Although the *Pipeline* was primarily designed for adult males, several thousand young women and children were detained in a camp in Kamiti. Babies were born in captivity, many got sick and died; women were humiliated and raped. These camps were later called a British gulag, and compared to Bergen-Belsen specifically—a chilling comparison considering that they existed within a decade of the liberation of the Nazi concentration camps.

By 1960, the official end of the conflict, the number of fatalities among Kenya's more than thirty thousand white settlers was surprisingly low: thirty-two dead and twenty-six wounded. By contrast, the Mau Mau murdered nearly two thousand African civilians and wounded close to another thousand. As for the Mau Mau, the number of those who were executed by the British or who died in the detention camps from torture, malnutrition, or disease—pulmonary tuberculosis was rampant—vary from an appalling fifteen thousand to a still more appalling thirty thousand.

Uli has known Bibi, the nurse-midwife on the sisal plantation, since Bibi was a child and it was she who urged Bibi to go to nursing school in Dar es Salaam. Now, Bibi delivers babies and tends to the sick—and tends to Uli, who comes down with malaria. Although not the life-threatening kind (*Plasmodium falciparum*), Uli's type of malaria parasites (*Plasmodium vivax*) causes first chills, then sweating and a high fever. Uli sweats through her nightdress, her sheets, soaking her mattress. And during the entire time—three wearisome days—Bibi, loyal and uncomplaining, never leaves Uli's bedside.

The European doctor comes in the late afternoon of the second day and prescribes chloroquine for Uli. Afterward, tired from his medical rounds, he joins Claus on the terrace. They each drink a glass of whiskey and watch the sun go down on the sisal fields.

"In the 1920s," the doctor tells Claus, "it was discovered that black Africans have an intrinsic resistance to malaria but no one knew why. It was not until a few years ago that researchers working in Madagascar found that a great number of the people they tested who had vivax malaria—the type of malaria Uli has—were Duffy-negative—"

"Duffy what?" Claus interrupts, frowning.

"The name comes from a hemophiliac whose serums contained the antibody, but what it means is that most African blacks lack the so-called Duffy proteins on the surfaces of their red blood cells to which the vivax malaria parasites attach, and that makes them immune."

Claus calls for Nyatta, one of the houseboys. Nyatta does not answer and Claus calls again, louder. When finally Nyatta arrives, Claus says, "Didn't you hear me?"

"No, bwana." Nyatta shakes his head.

Not sure whether to believe him, Claus asks Nyatta to bring

two more whiskeys, one for the doctor and one for him. When the drinks arrive, the two men sit in companionable silence. They can hear Nyatta and Andrea and the cook, Juma, in the kitchen, preparing the evening meal—sounds of water boiling, the clatter of pans, something frying being stirred. They can also hear the men talking to one another in Swahili.

"Do you trust them?" the doctor breaks the silence and asks softly, pointing toward the sounds with his chin. "You've heard, of course."

"Yes. Dreadful," Claus answers. "The poor Ruck family and that poor child."

As for the servants, how can he be sure, but he does not want to answer the doctor. He does not want to expose his growing unease—speaking of it will only make it worse. Instead he says, "Nyatta and Andrea are good boys. I've known them since they were children. They grew up on the estate."

Juma, the cook, has been a bit surly of late. Last night, the chicken was not cooked thoroughly enough—the meat at the joints was still pink. When Claus pointed this out, Juma shrugged his shoulders and said something about the stove not working properly. But Juma, Claus has also heard, is having wife problems, which may account for his bad mood. A few months before, Juma took another wife, a third wife, and his two other wives, who are older, resent the third wife. She is young and pretty and lazy.

At the thought, Claus shakes his head—Uli is wife enough for him.

"What is it, Claus?" the doctor asks, observing him.

"Juma is an excellent cook," Claus answers. "You should stay for dinner."

When Barbara finally arrived in the United States in the mid-fifties, she did not know whether to tell Irène that Rudy had lent her the money for the airfare. More than the airfare. And Rudy did not lend her the money, he had given it to her. He does not believe, he told her, in lending money. "It's the quickest way of losing a friend," he said, "You either give money or you don't, but you never loan it." Rudy was emphatic about this. "I also believe," he told Barbara, "that things come around. You never know. One day, someone may give me money when I need it."

She and Irène were sitting in the living room waiting for Gaby to come home for dinner. Gaby also had been generous to Barbara. He has sponsored Barbara and signed an affidavit that she would not become a public charge. In addition, he and Irène have offered to lend Barbara money while she went back to school and took refresher courses so that she could practice medicine again.

"I have enough for now," Barbara had told them.

"Don't worry, if I need more money, I'll ask," she also tells Irène, who had mentioned the loan again.

"Are you sure?"

"Yes. In fact . . ." Barbara hesitated. She prided herself on being honest. "In fact," she repeated, "Rudy gave me some money."

"Rudy gave you money?" Irène asked, surprised. "Why did Rudy give you money?"

"I ran into him in the street in Paris, with Tolia," Barbara started to explain. "You remember Tolia?"

"Yes, I remember Tolia," Irène said, frowning. "Tolia is a thief. Didn't he go to jail? But what has Tolia got to do with Rudy lending you money?" She sounded irritated.

"Nothing. Except that we had lunch at *Korniloff*, a Russian restaurant—"

"I know *Korniloff's*," Irène interrupts. "It was full of those impoverished White Russians forever whining about their lost titles and their estates. And I hated those heavy pirozhkis and blinis." Irène made a face.

"I told Rudy that I wanted to come to the States," Barbara continued, trying to ignore Iréne, "but I didn't have very much money and—"

"Stop! Don't tell me!" Irène had gotten up from her chair and, her hands on her hips, she stood in front of Barbara and asked, "Did you sleep with Rudy?"

Shocked, Barbara answered her in German, *"Nein, nein, Rehlein."*

"You did, didn't you? And, please speak English," Irène told Barbara.

"Of course, I didn't sleep with Rudy," Barbara says, close to tears. "Oh, Rehlein, you must believe me."

"I am not sure I do," Irène said. Shrugging her shoulders, she sat down again as the front door opened and Gaby came in.

"Good evening, ladies," he said. "How is my lovely wife and my lovely sister-in-law?" He sounded a little drunk. "I'm sorry I'm late, but I stopped off and had a drink with a client."

"Dinner is ready," Irène told him, "and I'm hungry. Come," she also says, holding out her hand to Barbara by way of apology, "you must be hungry as well."

Her freshman year in college, Liliane lives on campus in a large women's dormitory. An only child, she is not used to communal living. She resents having to do kitchen duty (hosing down greasy plates full of leftover food and carrying heavy trays) and the lack of privacy in the bathroom (often toilets are left unflushed and hairs clog the drains in the tubs), but the noise is worse: the constant shouting and screaming of overexcited girls on the stairs and in the hallways. Worse still, the public phone on Liliane's floor is right next to her room and it rings and rings and rings at all hours of the day and night and no one picks it up. Often, incapable of ignoring the sound any longer, Liliane goes out into the hall and, without answering it, takes the phone off the hook and lets the receiver dangle in the air.

Hello, hello, is— Liliane hears the faint sound of a male voice that is both hopeful and grateful that the phone at last has been answered and she takes a grim satisfaction knowing that he will be disappointed.

Although Liliane has gone to several social mixers and on a few dates, she does not yet have a boyfriend. The college boys she has met so far seem young and immature and she feels both superior and lonely. She does not like the rainy, cold New England weather and, except for the pretty houses along Brattle Street, she finds the town of Cambridge gray and dreary. Her principal mode of transportation is a bicycle and already she has gotten her wheel caught in a trolley track and, more dangerous still, has had a car door open brusquely in front of her. Once as she walks through the Cambridge Common to her class, a man sitting on a bench next to the commemorative plaque that marks the spot where George Washington is said to have stood when he first took command of the Continental Army during the Revolutionary War exposes himself to her.

Her classes are mostly core courses and required. Her least favorite is Natural Sciences 3, taught by Professor I. Bernard Cohen. The class of more than three hundred students meets twice a week, at nine o'clock in the morning in a vast auditorium. Professor Cohen is famous for his books on Benjamin Franklin and Isaac Newton; he is also famous for conducting experiments in class. The most memorable class demonstration involves sending a brass ball on a wire swinging between the heads of two teaching fellows to show the periodicity of a pendulum. Galileo Galilei was the first to observe that the bobs of pendulums nearly return to their release height, Professor Cohen explains. The time for one complete cycle, a left swing and a right swing, is called the period. A pendulum swings with a specific period that depends on its length. When given an initial push, it will swing back and forth at a constant amplitude. . . . After attending the first few lectures, Liliane does not bother to attend again. The midterm exam consists of multiple true and false questions and Liliane checks the answers arbitrarily—*true, true, true, false, false, true, true, true.* She fails the exam.

One night, when Liliane is already in bed and nearly asleep, the telephone starts to ring again. This time she is determined to try to drown out the sound by putting a pillow over her head. After a while, the phone stops ringing, then she hears someone knocking on her door.

"Lil," the person who is knocking calls out, "the phone is for you. It's your mother, she says it is urgent."

Rudy has had a massive stroke. The Italian doctor does not expect Rudy to live for more than a few hours. If Liliane wants to see her father alive, the Italian doctor says, she must come over right away. "*Subito, subito*" the doctor repeats, and Liliane is reminded of how, years ago, the maid, Maria, spoke to call her a taxi.

At Logan Airport in Boston, Liliane buys a ticket on the next flight to Rome. A TWA flight. Her seat is next to the window and looks out over the wing of the plane. It is early evening and already dark and Liliane, who does not like to fly, closes her eyes during the noisy takeoff. The plane is barely up in the air when Liliane hears what sounds like an explosion, then the woman seated behind her screams. Looking out her window, Liliane sees that one of the plane's engines has caught on fire. Orange flames light up the night sky. Across the aisle from Liliane a woman starts to cry softly; the rest of the passengers on the plane, however, are strangely quiet. Silently praying, Liliane stares out her window until the flames go out.

After several long minutes, the pilot's voice is heard reassuring the passengers that the fire has been extinguished and that every plane is equipped with a built-in firefighting mechanism to deal with just such a situation. As for the noise the passengers heard, the pilot explains—he speaks with a slight western drawl—it was caused not by an explosion but by the sudden vacuum created when the engine stalled. He then goes on to inform them that they will have to circle for a while over the Atlantic Ocean in order to dump fuel before they can safely return to Logan Airport and land.

They circle over the Atlantic Ocean dumping fuel for nearly an hour; then, when the plane has lowered its wheels and is getting ready to land, the pilot's laconic voice is again heard telling the passengers—"only as a precaution," he says—to place their pillows on their laps and put their heads down, for the women passengers to take off their high-heel shoes and for those wearing glasses to remove them. Again the cabin is quiet, except for the woman across the aisle from Liliane who starts to cry softly. The plane lands with an abrupt lurch and a squeal of brakes and when Liliane lifts her head from her pillow and looks out the window, she sees that the runway is lined with fire trucks.

Six hours later, Liliane is on another TWA flight to Rome. This time the plane flies smoothly in an almost cloudless light sky, the steel-gray ocean miles below. Again, Liliane has a window seat, but now she pulls down the window shade and closes her eyes. She would like to sleep and not to be afraid.

Not only his health but Rudy's film career has taken a turn for the worse. His co-productions starring the bodybuilder Steve Reeves as various biblical and mythological figures such as Hercules, Aeneas, and Goliath in what are mockingly referred to as sword-and-sandal epics proved a financial disappointment. (Reeves's career, too, was also brought up short when, while filming the remake of *The Last Days of Pompeii* and accustomed to doing his own stunts, he ran his chariot into a tree and dislocated his shoulder.) In addition, instead of saving his money, Rudy has either spent or given it all away. As a result, he has to play cards for a living and has, he claims, a standing game of gin rummy at Bricktop. But because of his failing eyesight and his swollen fingers, Liliane guesses, Rudy can no longer hold up the cards properly or see them clearly enough to win. This more than anything else causes her to already grieve for him.

By the time Liliane arrives in Rome, it is afternoon and too late; Rudy is dead.

XI

At Easter, during her junior year of college, Liliane drives from Cambridge to Ithaca to visit Emilie. It is the first time she has driven a long distance—330 miles—by herself and although she is a little apprehensive about getting lost, about getting a ticket for driving too fast, which she does, or worse, about perhaps denting a fender of her boyfriend's red MG, she also feels free. She could, she tells herself, keep driving—drive all the way to the West Coast or to Canada, to places she has never been. She also likes the feeling that no one—not her parents, not her friends, and, especially, not Mark, her boyfriend—knows precisely where she is at this moment.

Emilie no longer lives in her Stewart Avenue apartment, but lives in a nursing home. She is going to be ninety-three years old next month and she is very frail; this may be the last time Liliane sees her.

"Edith," Emilie says when Liliane walks into her room.

"No," Liliane answers gently, "it's me, Liliane, your granddaughter."

"Yes, I know," Emilie says. "Only sometimes I confuse things."

In a plain room in the nursing home, Emilie is lying in a hospital bed. The side bars are raised so she won't fall out. On a tray attached to the bed is a half-empty glass of water with a bent straw sticking out of it, a box of Kleenex, and a little worn-looking black book. A prayer book.

The other bed in the room is empty and, following Liliane's gaze, Emilie says, "The woman died a few days ago. She was colored. A nice lady," Emilie adds. "They asked me if I wanted to move," Emilie continues, "the bed is next to the window."

"Do you want to?" Liliane asks.

Emilie shrugs. "Is there anything to see?" Then in a stronger voice, she asks Liliane, "Do you know the story of the two soldiers?"

Pulling up a chair, Liliane sits next to Emilie's bed. "Tell me," she says.

"During the First World War, two wounded soldiers share a room in the hospital. The soldier who has the bed next to the window keeps regaling the other soldier with what he sees. He says he sees beautiful women walking by, and he describes what they look like—blondes, brunettes, redheads—and, of course, the soldier who is lying in the bed that is not next to the window becomes jealous and he, too, wants to be able to look out. So, one night, when the soldier who is in the bed next to the window takes a turn for the worse and begs the other soldier to fetch help, the soldier in the bed next to him ignores his anguished cries and lets the poor soldier die. The next day, after the body has been taken away and the nurse has made up the bed again, the soldier asks to be moved to the bed next to the window and when he finally gets to look out the window, do you know what he sees?"

"No," Liliane says, shaking her head.

"A brick wall."

After a moment, Liliane asks, "Is this a true story?"

But Emilie's eyes are closed and she does not answer.

Only then does Liliane remember the sepia photo she once saw of an unsmiling Emilie and several other women wearing nurses' uniforms, standing among a group of German officers.

When Emilie opens her eyes again, she says, "You know what I regret most in my life?"

"No," Liliane answers. "What?"

"That I let my mother die alone in Hamburg—remember I told you about Fides. Her real name was Friederike but everyone called her Fides."

Liliane remembers the story of Fides laughing when Rudolf fell off his horse and how he vowed never to see her again, yet he married her.

"It was so cruel," Emilie says. "I think about it all the time— how frightened and abandoned poor Fides must have felt."

"But if you had stayed in Hamburg, who knows what might have happened to you," Liliane says. "You might have been sent to one of the camps."

Instead Emilie picks up the worn-looking little black book on her tray and holds it out to Liliane. "Will you read me a prayer?" she asks.

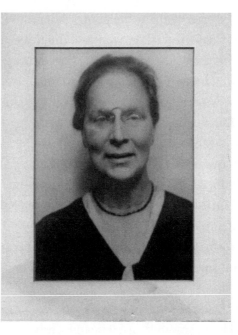

Crying as she backs Mark's MG out of the parking lot of the nursing home, Liliane does not see the oncoming van. Both a fender and a taillight are smashed.

Liliane first noticed Mark in Professor Perry Miller's class on *Moby-Dick* because he is tall and good-looking; at the same time, she dismisses him as a jock. Although she plans on reading *Moby-Dick*, she does not bother to attend many of the classes, but Mark, to his credit, does. He, too, has noticed Liliane and first approaches her as she is sitting in Hayes-Bickford, the coffee shop in Harvard Square, reading—not *Moby-Dick* but a book of Robert Lowell's poems: a first edition of *Lord Weary's Castle*, given her by a fellow student named Fred. In time, Fred, too, will become a well-known poet; at present, he has written a love poem comparing Liliane to a seal and another called *"The Love Letter,"* which ends with:

The mailman took the letter—
only at each step, under his broad chest
his lungs, as under a sidewalk, shook
like an unrecovered bomb, menacing everyone.

The boy went back to sleep.
The girl was a thousand miles away.

"I haven't seen you in class much" is how Mark begins.

Barely glancing up from her book, Liliane answers, "That's right. I haven't been."

"You should hear Professor Miller read," Mark continues, ignoring Liliane's tone. "He could be Captain Ahab." Then, standing in front of her in the coffee shop, he raises his arms in the air and begins to recite in a loud voice, *"Towards thee I roll, thou all-destroying but un-conquering whale; to the last I grapple with thee; from hell's heart I stab at thee—* Damn, I forget the rest," Mark says.

Putting aside the Robert Lowell poems, Liliane laughs and Mark, without waiting to be asked, sits down next to her and orders a cup of coffee.

Liliane likes his lack of inhibition, his energy, his spontaneity—all qualities she feels she lacks. She also likes driving in his red MG with the top down. Some nights, they go into Boston for dinner—besides being tall and good-looking, Mark is rich—or, if the night is warm enough, they go to Revere Beach, where he parks in a secluded spot and, after they have spread out the plaid blanket he keeps in the trunk of his car, they make hurried love on the beach.

Finding a place to make love is a challenge. Liliane lives in a small off-campus house and has a roommate; Mark lives in Eliot House and has three roommates and although he sometimes manages to arrange for all three of them to be out, Liliane is reluctant to go there. Mark's suite of rooms is a mess— dirty clothes lie on the floor along with empty beer bottles, glasses, food wrappers—and Mark's bed is unmade, the sheets unchanged for weeks, perhaps months. Also, she worries that a roommate will walk in on them and, nervous, while she and Mark are making love, she fakes having an orgasm. Most times with him, anyway, Liliane fakes it.

Liliane offers to pay for the smashed fender and taillight but Mark says there is no need. In a month, he will graduate from college and his parents, as a graduation gift, have offered him a trip around the world; he will sell the MG—smashed fender, taillight, and all.

"I'll start in Japan," Mark tells Liliane, "then Hong Kong, and from there"—Mark pauses a moment—"I want to go to Vietnam. My dad knows Elbridge Durbrow, the U.S. ambassador to South Vietnam, and he said he'll write him a letter and maybe I can stay at the embassy for a couple of days. According to my dad, Durbrow is having a rough time with Diem."

"Gaby, my stepfather, keeps talking about the domino theory," Liliane says, wanting to sound informed. She pictures an infinite row of black dominoes toppling one on top of the other.

"From Vietnam, I'll go to Thailand," Mark continues.

"Siam," Liliane interjects—she much prefers the country's former name.

"I want to meet Jim Thompson—the American who lives in Bangkok. Apparently, he parachuted into Thailand during World War II, fell in love with the country, and never left. Besides his Thai silk business, he is supposed to have a beautiful collection of Asian art."

"He sounds—"

"Then I'll probably go to India," Mark says, not letting Liliane finish. "A friend of mine knows a maharaja in Jaipur who can organize a tiger shoot. You should come with me, Lil," he adds as an afterthought, taking Liliane in his arms. "Think of all the adventures we will have."

In early June, Gaby collapses in the street while eating a hot dog. Apparently, he dies instantly from a massive heart attack while walking down Park Avenue. He had just come from the dentist and since he did not have time to have lunch at his club, he had bought a hot dog from a street vendor. The attack occurred a few blocks from Lenox Hill Hospital, where he was taken to the emergency room, but according to the attending doctor, it was too late—the unchewed hot dog still in Gaby's mouth.

"Please stay, *chérie*," Irène, distraught, pleads with Liliane. "Don't go to work. I need you."

Her grief is genuine and intense and Liliane does not know how to try to comfort her mother. She is not glad Gaby is dead but neither is she sad.

The apartment is filled with baskets of fruits, casseroles, flowers; letters of condolence arrive; the phone rings—a constant outpouring of sympathy, but Irène is not consoled.

The funeral parlor is located a few blocks from the apartment, but Irène refuses to go. She does not want to see Gaby—
she does not want to remember him that way, she says, tearfully.
Instead, she chooses the clothes—a blue blazer, gray slacks, a
green-and-white club tie—for him to be cremated in and Liliane
takes them to the funeral parlor. Three days later, Liliane goes
back again to identify Gaby—a state law apparently—before he
is cremated. The coffin is open and Liliane takes such a quick
look that it could have been anyone inside, she realizes later.
She, too, does not want to see Gaby again.

After Irène has left the city for the island in Penobscot
Bay, Liliane again stays in the apartment alone. She has a summer job working for a small nonprofit organization. Again, she
files, types—she is a better typist now—and answers the phone.
Arthur, her boss, is young and affable. He takes her out to lunch
and they eat outdoors in the sun at the Central Park Zoo cafeteria. The lunches grow longer and longer; afterward, they go for
a walk together, like a couple, and look at the animals in their
cages—the hot polar bears.

"No one is in the office to answer the phone." Liliane cannot help but be concerned.

"They'll call back if it is important," Arthur answers.

When, one time, he asks her out for dinner, Liliane tells
him she has a steady boyfriend.

"But we can have lunch, right?" Arthur says.

The memorial service for Gaby takes place in August in the
church on the island in Penobscot Bay and Liliane takes two days
off from work to go. She will fly up to the nearest airport, then

take a taxi to the ferry terminal. Before she leaves, however, she has to pick up Gaby's cremains from the funeral parlor. She has promised Irène that she will bring them on the plane.

Gaby's cremains are inside a brown paper shopping bag that is taped shut. The bag is surprisingly heavy and, as Liliane walks back to the apartment, she holds it out, not letting the bag touch her side. She also hopes that she will not run into anyone she knows, afraid the person might ask, *What's in the bag?* In spite of herself, the thought makes her giggle.

On her way, Liliane walks by a dress store—a sign in the window announces a sale—and she goes inside. The dress is white linen with a scooped neck and dark blue piping around the neck, the armholes, and the side seams, and when she tries it on in the dressing room, the dress fits perfectly.

"Is it for a special occasion?" The saleslady wants to know.

"Yes, a wedding," Liliane lies.

After several blocks walking home again, holding the package with her new dress inside it, Liliane, all of a sudden, realizes that she has left the bag with the cremains on the floor of the dressing room. Breaking out into a cold sweat, she runs back to the store.

What, she thinks, *if someone found the bag and threw it out or, worse, took it* and *what,* she also thinks, *will she tell Irène?*

Fortunately, the bag is still where she left it and, relieved, Liliane starts to explain to the saleslady. "I'm sorry, I forgot—"

Forgot what? Her stepfather.

The church is packed. Gaby was a well-known and well-liked summer resident on the island. He sailed, played tennis and golf; he was a permanent member of the yacht club committee. Relatives have come from all over the country to attend the memorial service, including Irène's sister Barbara, who has come from Newport, Rhode Island.

Sitting in the front row pew, Irène is dressed in black and looks elegant. Next to her, Liliane is wearing her new white dress. Earlier, afraid that Irène might object to the dress and find it too showy, Liliane tried to reassure her by saying, "In many countries, white is considered the color of mourning."

Irène's distant ancestor, Mary, Queen of Scots, wore white after the deaths of her father-in-law, her mother, and her first husband, Francis II of France. *Deuil blanc* (white mourning), as the custom was called, was the color of the deepest mourning for European queens—purple was worn by kings. White is also the color of mourning in India, Vietnam, and South Korea; traditionally, too, white clothes and hats are worn by the Chinese at their funerals. The color white—as opposed to black, associated by early Christians with the color of the universe before God created light and with ignorance and paganism—evokes the paleness of death, celestial light, and everlasting life according to certain cultures who believe in the immortality of the soul.

Gaby's service begins with the minister reading: "*I am the resurrection and the life,*" *says the Lord.* "*Those who believe in me, even though they die, will live, and everyone who lives and believes in me will never die.*"

Barbara is sitting on the other side of Irène; she wears a plain navy blue dress. When the service begins, she reaches over and takes Irène's hand in hers and holds it.

Standing up, the congregation sings:
Holy, Holy Holy! Lord God Almighty!

Gaby's nephew, a boy of twelve, walks to the front of the church and stands behind the lectern and, in a trembling voice, reads Psalm 23.

The Lord is my shepherd; I shall not want.
He maketh me to lie down in green pastures:
he leadeth me beside the still waters.

Two of Gaby's closest friends one after the other go up to the lectern to speak. Men much like Gaby in background and upbringing, each has known Gaby since he was a small boy, in the case of one of the men, since Gaby was born—here on the island and elsewhere. They each tell amusing stories about Gaby—mishaps involving alcohol and automobiles at school and at college—how Gaby misbehaved but got away with it. They speak of his charm, his wit, his generosity, his courage during the war—the incident when Gaby's ship the USS *Ingraham* collided with the oil tanker *Chemung* in thick fog off the coast of Nova Scotia and how Gaby and a half dozen other men survived for thirty-six hours in a lifeboat before they were rescued—his love of sports, sailing especially, his love of life, his love of family: in particular, his beautiful wife, Irène, as well as his stepdaughter, Lillian.

Although she has begged Irène that she does not want to, that she is shy, that she is not a good public speaker, and, finally and, perhaps, most compellingly, that she does not like the Tennyson poem—which, she declares, is sentimental and maudlin—Liliane cannot dissuade Irène, and she is next. Standing at the lectern, Liliane reads Gaby's favorite poem:

Sunset and evening star,
   And one clear call for me!
And may there be no moaning of the bar,
   When I put out to sea.

The congregation recites the Apostles' Creed, then the Lord's Prayer; the minister gives the Blessing; they sing one more hymn, "Amazing Grace"; and, at last, the minister offers the Nunc Dimittis:

Lord, now lettest thou thy servant depart in peace: according to thy word
and Gaby's memorial service is over. Irène, Barbara, and Liliane walk out together to the rousing organ sounds of Charles-Marie Widor's Toccata from Symphony no. 5.

A reception in the summer house follows. Local island people are hired to help out—a bartender and two maids to pass hors d'oeuvres and clean up afterward. It is a bright sunny day— almost a fall day, the air is clear and crisp—and, drinks in hand, people spill out onto the lawn. At first the conversations and remarks stay muted, quiet, but then as people drink and eat more—cheese puffs and little crabmeat sandwiches—they relax and talk louder, tell jokes, laugh. Soon the reception sounds like any other island cocktail party and Gaby, it would appear—or his death—seems to be momentarily forgotten.

Liliane talks to Christine and Porter. Porter spent the winter in Aspen working as a ski lift operator—according to what he tells Liliane and Christine, he is still trying to find himself.

Carlton has joined the Marines and will be killed a few years later on New Year's Eve, when his helicopter gunship is shot down and crashes in the Quang Giao rubber plantation, about four kilometers from Bình Gia. Missy got pregnant and had to get married. The baby, a boy, was born two weeks ago, Christine tells Liliane, and weighed ten pounds. Phyllis is hitchhiking through Europe by herself. Christine is engaged to Jackson, who is in law school. Putting out her left hand, she shows Liliane her ring—a small emerald with a baguette diamond on either side of it.

"Emeralds are highly included," Christine says. "I have to be careful and take the ring off when I do dishes and stuff."

Holding a glass of tomato juice into which she has poured a shot of vodka, Liliane goes outside. She is looking for her aunt Barbara. She finds her sitting on the grass by herself, smoking a cigarette and looking out to sea.

"It's beautiful here," Barbara says when Liliane—hesitating at first, as she does not want to get grass stains on her new dress—sits down beside her. "No wonder Gaby loved this place so much."

Looking over, Barbara asks, "Are you all right? I mean about Gaby."

For a moment, Liliane is tempted to tell Barbara how, a few summers ago, Gaby would come into her room at night and lie on top of her.

"Can I have a cigarette?" she says instead.

"A bad habit," Barbara says, handing Liliane her packet of cigarettes and her lighter.

"Here, have some of this," Liliane tells Barbara, offering her the glass of vodka and tomato juice.

"But you look wonderful," Barbara says after she has drunk a little of the tomato juice and vodka. "I've never seen you look so well and that is such a pretty dress," she adds.

"You must be in love," Barbara says with a smile.

To try to make up for lost time her senior year, Liliane attends classes, does the reading, writes papers on time, and gets good grades. Every afternoon, she studies in Widener Library. The Harry Elkins Widener Memorial Library was built in 1915 to commemorate the death of Harry Elkins Widener on board the *Titanic*. Harry, his mother, Eleanor, and his father, George, along with Eleanor's maid, Amalie Gieger, and George's valet, Edwin Keeping, were returning from a book-collecting trip in London when the ship hit the iceberg. George and Harry accompanied Eleanor and Amalie to a lifeboat, then chose to take their chances and remain on board, where, along with Edwin, they perished. As soon as she was back home in Philadelphia, Eleanor gave Harvard two million dollars to build the library in memory of her son, Harry. The building houses over fifty miles of bookshelves and more than three million volumes, including copies of the first folio of Shakespeare and the Gutenberg Bible.

According to popular legend, Eleanor Widener's donation rested on the condition that all Harvard men and women know how to swim before they graduate—the ability, she no doubt thought, might have saved her son's life. Liliane, along with her fellow freshmen, were required to take a swimming test. The test was easy—a few laps back and forth in a pool—and not a problem, but she also had to have her photo taken nude. At the time, except for feeling embarrassed, she had not thought much about it and it was not until many years later that objections were raised about the practice.

The purpose of the nude posture photos taken from the 1940s through the 1970s of all incoming freshmen at certain Ivy League colleges was ostensibly to gauge the occurrence and severity of rickets, scoliosis, and lordosis in the student population. However, the project, which was overseen by William Herbert Sheldon, a psychologist and numismatist, and Earnest Albert Hooton, an anthropologist, was in fact designed to support their theory on how body types can reveal intelligence, moral value, and future accomplishment.

"From the outset," according to Hooton, "the purpose of these 'posture photographs' was eugenic. The data accumulated will eventually lead on to proposals to 'control and limit the production of inferior and useless organisms.' Some of the latter would be penalized for reproducing . . . or would be sterilized. But the real solution is to be enforced better breeding—getting those Exeter and Harvard men together with their corresponding Wellesley, Vassar and Radcliffe girls."

The questions remain: Were the colleges at the time complicit or were they duped by that posture photo study? And what happened to all those photos? And more troublesome still is the thought that the Nazis, not so long before, made similar studies, amassing photographs and analyzing them for racial and characterological information in order to justify the eventual murder of six million people.

*   *   *

Sitting in Widener Library's immense reading room, Liliane tries to rework her novel about Heathcliff. Instead of having the narrator and Heathcliff live together in the desolate English countryside, now—inspired by Mark's letters from the Far East— she has them travel to India.

> *The voyage from Liverpool to Calcutta takes forty days.*
> *During that time they encounter all the extremes of weather:*
> *frigid cold as they navigate around the Cape of Good Hope,*
> *tossed violently about by both the Atlantic and the Indian*
> *Oceans, and intense suffocating heat as, twice, they cross the*
> *equator—along the west coast and again on the east coast of*
> *Africa. The ship is foul; the food nearly inedible—dried pork,*
> *rotted potatoes, moldy raisins—the crew surly and mutinous.*
> *I am seasick during most of the voyage, but Heathcliff seems*
> *to thrive on salt air and squalls. Even during the worst of*
> *them, he stays out, his feet firmly planted on the deck, his*
> *body braced against the mast, and laughs.*

Mark writes Liliane from Tokyo and Kyoto, from Hong Kong and Saigon—on American embassy stationery—and most recently, from the Oriental Hotel in Bangkok. His letters are well written and descriptive. From his hotel window, he describes how he can watch the boats going back and forth across the Chao Phrya River; he also writes how the Bangkok streets are lined with flame-of-the-forest trees, frangipani and bougainvillea; how graceful and attractive the Thai people are—always smiling—and how hospitable. Including Jim Thompson. Already, Mark has dined at his house twice— sitting out on the terrace and watching the silk weavers across the *klong*—*klong*, Mark writes, is the Thai word for "canal." Jim Thompson has suggested that they go up-country together to explore caves that are reputed to be filled with statues. "This country," Mark writes, "as you can imagine—for I do credit you with an imagination, even though you persist in saying that you have none—is full of wonderful opportunities, unexplored regions—"

Pausing, Liliane reflects how, instinctively, perhaps not to alarm Mark with her intellectual pursuits or goals, she has never told him that she is writing a novel and that she reads poetry for pleasure.

"What are you thinking about?" Mark, from time to time, asks her. No doubt, he intuits that Liliane is concealing something important from him.

"Nothing," Liliane tells him.

The letter continues: "I think of you being here a great deal and spend long periods imagining how both of us would feel. I hope very much you will decide to come to Bangkok and I don't think I will be dragging a pair of sore feet around or that you will be any sort of burden."

Fifty years earlier, on their honeymoon, Mark's newlywed aunt and husband rode from Bangkok to Rangoon on elephant back. It took them three months.

Mark ends his letter by again urging Liliane to join him: "I want you to come very badly, Lil. Thailand is a marvelously warm and distant place."

Bangkok is one of the hottest cities in the world. From March to May, the temperature soars to 105 humid degrees Fahrenheit. The tar roads in the city melt and are littered with stuck shoes pedestrians have left in their hurry to cross.

Rereading the last lines of Mark's letter, Liliane packs a small suitcase in her head: a few skirts, two or three T-shirts, jeans, a pair of sturdy sandals. She will travel light and not be a burden.

Liliane's favorite class is taught by Professor Paul de Man. Born in Antwerp, Belgium, in 1919, Paul de Man immigrated to the United States after the war (and after he translated *Moby-Dick* into Dutch) and taught first at Bard College before he obtained a junior fellowship at Harvard—a prestigious award given to scholars whose work holds exceptional promise. His class is a graduate seminar on allegory in the French poets: Baudelaire, Rimbaud, and Mallarmé. (Given her lackluster college record, Liliane is not quite sure how she was admitted to this exclusive class, except, perhaps, for the fact that she speaks fluent French.) Blond with Teutonic good looks and remarkably bright blue eyes, Paul de Man is mild-mannered and soft-spoken. He begins the seminar by quoting Blaise Pascal, "*Quand on lit trop vite ou trop doucement on n'entend rien*"—When one reads too quickly or too slowly, one hears nothing.

"Allegory," de Man continues, "as we all know, is a literary figure where one thing refers to something else. A dove is the classical example. In a poem a dove is an allegory of peace but the reader also right away recognizes that a dove is a bird although in the poem it refers to something else. All narratives are allegories because of the gap that occurs between what the narrative does not say and what the reader does not say—a gap, in other words, between reference and referent. This gap leads to a misreading and misreading is an integral part of meaning. Meaning, in fact, relies on misreading; meaning is always plural."

The seminar meets once a week for two hours in a classroom on the third floor of Sever Hall. It is made up of ten students—most of them graduate students and most of them male—all of whom are ambitious, immersed in their work, and pay no attention to the undergraduate Liliane. Busy taking notes—she can't write fast enough—Liliane does not notice them either. For class, she reads Baudelaire's dark confessional ruminations of *Les Fleurs du mal*, Rimbaud's rebellious, deranged verse of *Le Bateau ivre* as well as the exhilarating and confounding prose poems of *Illuminations*.

Instead of an exam, the students in de Man's seminar are required to write a term paper. Liliane chooses to write a paper on Mallarmé's three "Éventail"—Fan—poems. Working on it for weeks, she steeps herself deeply into the text, examining the French words, *calice, fiole,* the rhymes, *plonge, mensonge* the homophones, *apparaisse, sans paresse.* "The subject of the first "Éventail" poem," she writes, "is Mallarmé's wife's fan and it begins with the line *Avec comme pour langage*—With as for language—and it is those three linked prepositions that will establish the relationship between the language and the beating of the fan." In the second stanza, the poet sees the beating reflected in a mirror, and through the process of reflection sees it become solidified into a wing. "The fan," Liliane writes, "is a reflection and not a real fan, and the beating is the Idea of beating and not the beating itself."

"How does one distinguish literary language from ordinary language? And when does journalism become literature and when does memoir become literary?" de Man asks the seminar students as he walks over and leans on Liliane's desk to make his point. "The specificity of language rests in rhetoric. Rhetoric is the classical art of eloquence; it is associated with false and flowery language—tropes, metaphors, similes, and so forth. A rhetorical question is a question that does not require an answer and is therefore not a serious question. My point is that I believe all language—whether literary or ordinary—to be rhetorical, and rhetoric, by its very nature, deconstructs any presence of authenticity or reliability in the text."

Paul de Man is standing so close to Liliane that if she were to move her arm just a fraction she would touch his. She can also smell his aftershave, a vetiver scent, and a faint trace of tobacco—Gauloises, she imagines—and something else she cannot quite place that makes her think of starched shirts. Keeping her head bent, she does not dare look up at him as he talks, afraid it will distract her from understanding what he is saying:

1. Deconstruction allows for the other to speak.
2. Deconstruction opens the text out to an affirmation of the absence of fixed meaning.
3. Deconstruction is opposed to binary thinking where one term is privileged over another i.e., Man/Woman, West/East.
4. Deconstruction involves placing oneself inside the text.
5. Deconstruction questions the legitimacy of any closed system.
6. Deconstruction posits that nothing happens outside of the text.
7. Deconstruction posits that there is nothing but context.

*   *   *

"The premise of the second poem, 'Autre Éventail'—Another Fan," Liliane writes, "whose subject is the fan of Mallarmé's daughter rests on the difference between Mme Mallarmé and Mlle Mallarmé—the one a woman, the other a young girl. The poem begins: *O rêveuse, pour que je plonge*—Dreamer, that I may plunge—and Mlle Mallarmé is described as a dreamer, living in an imaginary world. Here, again, as in the first 'Éventail' poem, the movement of the fan is a wing—signifying the concept of movement, rather than movement itself."

The subject of the third "Éventail" poem is the fan of Mallarmé's mistress, Méry Laurent. Only Méry Laurent is dead. "The movement of the fan," Liliane writes, "is controlled by the poet's Idea of Méry's presence, which, since she is no longer alive, is impossible. The paradox inherent in this attempt parallels that of the act of poetic creation, where the attempt to create the poem distinct from language fails by virtue of the language itself on which the poem remains dependent."

In his next letter to Liliane, sent from Calcutta, Mark—because he may be lonely or the tiger shoot was a disappointment—declares himself more ardently to her: "I love you so much and am so very much in love with you and I want to share everything I know and think and believe with you. But I am a sentimental fool and at the moment I am all drawn up inside with the memory, feel, smell, touch, want, and passion for you and knowing how strongly I feel, I ask this one thing of you, if you have fallen out of love with me let me know."

The depth of feeling and the passionate tone in the letter takes Liliane by surprise. She misses Mark—his enthusiasms, his physical presence, even the rides in the red MG with the top down—but, absorbed writing her Mallarmé paper, she had neglected to answer his last letter. If only, she thinks, Mark knew what she was thinking:

> O rêveuse, pour que je plonge
> Au pur délice sans chemin,
> Sache, par un subtil mensonge,
> Garder mon aile dans ta main.

> Dreamer, that I may plunge
> In sweet and pathless pleasure,
> Understand how, by ingenious deceit,
> To keep my wing within your hand.

Then, frowning, she rereads part of Mark's letter—the part where he writes "if you have fallen out of love with me let me know"—afraid she has misread its meaning.

Although Liliane is in Professor de Man's thrall, she has had little personal contact with him. A few times, near the end of a seminar, as he is putting his papers back in his briefcase and preparing to leave, she gets up the courage to ask him a question. A question about rhyme in Baudelaire or why Rimbaud stopped writing when he was twenty years old. But most of her questions have to do with an assignment and, later, about when the term paper is due and Professor de Man has always answered her kindly and a bit abstractedly—smiling but not really looking at her. Always, too, he addresses her politely, by her family name. If, by chance, their paths cross in the Yard, as they are pushing their bicycles along, they nod and say hello, but do not stop. Once, in Cambridge, out on a date, Liliane sees Paul de Man having dinner at the French restaurant Henri IV. He is sitting next to a woman with long brown hair—her back is to Liliane—and another couple. Everyone at the table is drinking wine and having a good time. Liliane is not sure whether de Man sees her; he gives no sign that he does.

Paul de Man opened Liliane's mind and took her seriously; more specifically, he taught her how to read closely, how to intuitively interpret difficult texts, and how to view the authenticity of language. At the time, she, of course, had no idea that years later, and, mercifully, after his death, Professor de Man's reputation would be badly tarnished by his association to articles he was discovered to have written during World War II for *Le Soir,* a Belgian collaborationist newspaper; in particular, a single damning one titled "The Jews in Contemporary Literature," in which he posited that, without Jewish writers, literature would suffer no great loss. This revelation would spawn several more accusations—Paul de Man as a bigamist, as a forger, a liar, a swindler, a thief—all of which Liliane will find hard to believe. Impossible, really.

Professor de Man ends the seminar by repeating that deconstruction is the self-reflexive moment in a text when language both presents a figure of speech or trope and begins to undo or deconstruct it. This deconstruction occurs in all texts, even in autobiographical texts, and he mentions Rousseau's *Confessions*, Wordsworth's *The Prelude*, and Proust, saying that in À *la recherche du temps perdu*, which is meant to be autobiographical, it is impossible to tell what is fact and what is fiction. In fact, de Man continues, it is impossible to know whether figuration produces reference in a text or whether reference produces the figure. In any event, de Man says, warming to his subject, "Autobiography occurs when it involves two persons building their identities through reading each other. This requires a form of substitution—exchanging the writing 'I' for the written 'I'—and this also implies that both persons are at least as different as they are the same." The Memorial Church bell rings the hour, signaling the end of class, and nearly drowns out Professor de Man's last words: "In this way, I consider autobiography as an act of self-restoration in which the author recovers the fragments of his or her life into a coherent narrative."

Professor de Man gives Liliane an A on her Mallarmé paper on the three "Éventail" poems. "This is quite remarkable," he writes and, "I would like to hear what you are working on next!"

The flight to Bangkok takes sixteen hours and since they are flying at night, west, they never catch up with the sun. The whole time it stays dark. Somewhere over the Pacific, Liliane is not sure when exactly—each time the plane lands to refuel, she has to put her watch forward, first two hours, then three, then three more—or where exactly, maybe over the island of Wake or farther south over the island of Guam. When at last the plane lands at

The Three "Éventail" Poems of Mallarmé.

that is perhaps a little more obvious no The most general distinction between the three Mallarmé
*nothing-*poems entitled "Éventail" is that each one deals with the fan
of a different person: in the first, it is the fan of his wife,
Madame Mallarmé; in the second, that of his daughter, Mademoiselle Mallarmé; and in the third, that of a famous mistress, *where mistress?*
Méry. Each of these three women, by virtue of the nature of
their relationship to the poet, controls the subject of the
poem in the same sense that her action controls the movement
of the fan.

The first of these poems concerns the fan of Madame Mallarmé
in which it is clear from the first stanza that the movement of
the fan is the language from which the verse, the actual poem,
will emanate. The poem begins: "Avec comme pour langage", and
it is those three prepositions linked together which establish
the relationship between the language and the movement, or beating of the fan. The beating itself is nothing, ("rien"), it
produces only air, but a beating towards the skies. "Le futur
vers se dégage" suggests that the process of the creation of
the verse is similar to that of a butterfly emerging from its

Don Mueang Airport, it is bright day. They have crossed the
international date line and lost a day entirely. During the flight,
Liliane has hardly slept and her feet are so swollen she cannot
put her new red shoes back on. She has to walk barefoot across
the hot Thai tarmac holding her shoes in one hand. Looking up,
she half expects to see the lost day resting on a bank of clouds
float slowly away and out of her reach.

Epilogue

Chapter I

Venice of the East is how Claire's guidebook describes Bangkok and their house is on a canal, a klong. *The* klong *leads to a large outdoor market called Pratoo Nam and Claire can go there by boat. From the terrace of the house, she can hail one like a taxi and pay only a tical that rhymes with nickel—its worth. The taxi boat is a slender hull of teak with an outboard engine and a long propeller shaft that the boatman has to lift out of the water to avoid other boats, refuse, whatever else is floating in the canal. Often a dead dog is floating in the canal. Bloated, brown, pink, black, and terrible, the dog bobs up and down gently, ready to burst.*

The other passengers in the taxi boat are slender Siamese women wrapped like parcels in their red, blue, yellow sarongs.

*They ignore the dead dogs and, unless the boat becomes
unusually crowded, avoid sitting next to Claire.*

*"Falang, falang"—foreigner, foreigner—the women tell
one another in their singsong voices—"falang, falang."*

*Pratoo Nam market is large and, at first, Claire is afraid
of losing herself among the mangoes, the papayas, the litchis,
the pineapples and coconuts, the limes piled almost as high
as she, the twenty-six varieties of bananas, the fish, the squid
and octopus from the Bay of Siam, the spinach leaves, the
bunches of onions, the clumps of garlic, the live poultry and
the hundred-year-old black duck eggs soaked in horses' urine.*

*Bpai nai?—Where are you going? The vendors call out to
her. When they see her, they double their prices.*

Twenty-two, tall, blonde, Claire is easy to see.

*At home, all their food is prepared in a hot pepper sauce
by the cook, Lamum.*

*"The peppers kill the parasites," her husband, James, says.
He is proud that he eats local food and is not sick from it.
The food burns Claire's mouth, her throat, her stomach, later
her ass. With her chopsticks, Claire picks at her meal, shov-
ing aside the peppers, the seeds. "The smaller they are, the
hotter," James warns her. Claire's plate is a mess.*

*The kitchen is the home of ugly water rats. Claire has
seen Lamum throw a piece of burning charcoal at one. The
pots and pans are kept in a screened cupboard; the legs of
the cupboard are set in dishes of water so that the ants can't
crawl up. There are no appliances; the stove is two charcoal
pits. There is no sink; the cold water from a single spigot runs
directly onto the cement floor.*

Noi, the maid, has a baby boy. Except for a silver net that he wears over his penis, he is always naked. He is frightened of Claire, of how she looks. Each time he sees her, he starts to cry. At night, to put him to sleep, Noi masturbates him.

The back of the house—where Lamum, Noi, and Prachi, the houseboy, live—is a jungle of banana trees with their large messy leaves and all the garbage Lamum and Noi collect: empty bottles, wire hangers, tin cans. And there is always somebody else, somebody new, somebody Claire has never seen before. A cousin? An aunt? A younger brother? As far as Claire knows, she and James are supporting an entire family, an entire village. And didn't she once see a horse back there? Or did she dream this? Best not to ask. Best not to get involved, James says.

The front of the house is neat. The mowed green grass, the bougainvillea, the frangipani, the rosebushes that Claire plants. But because of the heat or the bugs, the roses do not bloom.

The swimming pool, too, is in the front of the house.

"We are not naturally immune as they are," Claire tells James about the water. She and James drink bottled water.

In the morning, as they breakfast on the terrace, they watch a woman bathe in the canal. The woman brushes her teeth, then she soaps her face, her neck, her arms; she soaps underneath her sarong. When she is through, she pulls a clean sarong over the old one without ever exposing any flesh.

"All these months and I still haven't seen her tits," James says.

"I don't understand why they are not all sick," Claire says. "I don't understand why they are not all dead. That water is indescribably filthy."

Acknowledgments

For statistics and information about the Italian working   17
class after World War II, I am indebted to *A History of Contemporary Italy: Society and Politics, 1943–1988* (New York:
Palgrave Macmillan, 2003), by Paul Ginsborg.

Quotations from Moses Mendelssohn are from Michah   82
Gottlieb, ed., *Moses Mendelssohn: Writings on Judaism, Chris-
tianity, and the Bible* (Waltham, Mass.: Brandeis University
Press, 2011).

For the story about Moses Mendelssohn's meeting with   81
Fromet Guggenheim, I am indebted to the site www.
wisdomportal.com/Romance/Mendelssohn-Gugenheim.
html; its source is Herbert Kuferberg; *The Mendelssohns:
Three Generations of Genius* (New York: Scribner, 1972).

The quotation about concentration-camp survivors is by   84
Dr. Yael Danieli, in an article by Gustav Niebuhr, "Painful
Nazi Era Legacy: Hidden Personal Histories of Survivors,"
The New York Times, February 5, 1997.

For the description of Mary, Queen of Scots' beheading, I   85
am indebted to Antonia Fraser's *Mary Queen of Scots* (1970;
repr., New York Delta/Bantam Dell Doubleday, 1993).

For facts about Josephine Baker's life, I am indebted to   86
Phyllis Rose's *Jazz Cleopatra: Josephine Baker in Her Time*
(New York: Vintage, 1991). The Josephine Baker "rear end"
quote comes from *Les Mémoires de Joséphine Baker* by Marcel Sauvage. Paris: Corréa, 1949.

For Anna Freud's theories on young girls' obsession with   91
horses, I am indebted to Deborah Bright's: "Horse Crazy,"
in *Horse Tales: American Images and Icons, 1800–2000* (Katonah, N.Y.: Katonah Museum of Art, 2001).

For information about Panagra Airline and flights over   50
the Andes, I am indebted to William A. Krusen, *Flying the
Andes* (Tampa: University of Tampa Press, 1997).

For information to describe Claude's exploits as a pilot dur-   137
ing World War Two, I am indebted to René Mouchotte,
The Mouchotte Diaries, ed. André Dezarrois, trans. Philip
Joun Stead (Bristol, U.K.: Cerberus, 2005), and to Pierre
Clostermann, *The Big Show: The Greatest Pilot's Story of
World War II* (London: Cassell Military Paperbacks, 2004).

Moravia's reminiscences are adapted from Alberto Moravia   171
and Alain Elkann, *Life of Moravia*, trans. William Weaver
(Hanover, N.H.: Steerforth Italia, 2000).

Frederick Seidel's poem "The Love Letter" appeared in *The*   213
Atlantic Monthly, June 1960, pp. 142–146.

The quotation about Earnest Hooten's purpose for the pos-   223
ture photographs is from Ron Rosenbaum, "The Great Ivy
League Nude Posture Photo Scandal," *The New York Times,*
January 15, 1995.

For Paul de Man's Harvard seminar, I have either quoted or   226
paraphrased Martin McQuillan's definition of allegory, his
definition of deconstruction, and his definition of autobiog-
raphy as de-facement and fiction from Martin McQuillan,
Paul de Man (London: Routledge, 2001) and from Paul de
Man, *Allegories of Reading: Figural Language in Rousseau,*
Nietzsche, Rilke, and Proust (New Haven: Yale University
Press, 1979).

I have quoted from Stéphane Mallarmé, *Collected Poems*   227
and Other Verse, trans. E. H. and A. M. Blackmore (Oxford:
Oxford University Press, 2006).

I also want to acknowledge and thank Katie Raissian and
Charles Rue Woods for their attention and work on my
behalf.